THE WITCHES OF SCOTLAND

THE DREAM DANCERS: AKASHIC CHRONICLES - BOOK 8

STEVEN P AITCHISON

CYT MEDIA LTD

This novel's story and characters are fictitious. Certain long-standing institutions, agencies and public offices are mentioned, as are street names, but the characters involved are wholly imaginary.

Steven Aitchison

The Witches of Scotland

The Dream Dancers: Akashic Chronicles Book 8

ISBN: 978-1915524102

FOLLOW AND LIKE

TIKTOK PAGE: www.tiktok.com/@steven_p_aitchison

AUTHOR: www.facebook.com/groups/stevenaitchisonauthor

FACEBOOK PAGE: www.facebook.com/ChangeYourThoughtsToday

EMAIL: authorsteven@stevenaitchison.co.uk

GET MORE URBAN FANTASY BOOK RECOMMENDATIONS

Urban Fantasy Book Club:

https://urban-fantasy-books.beehiiv.com/subscribe

Hey there, devoted readers of "The Witches of Scotland" series!

This dedication is for you, the awesome magickal readers who've been with me through all seven books. Your support on TikTok, Facebook, and email messages has been amazing, and chatting with you is the highlight of my day. I've tried to get back to each of you, but wow, your messages keep flooding in, so forgive me if I haven't gotten back to you yet.

So, we're at the last book in this series, and I can't quite believe we've got it here. After book two, I nervously paced my office, wondering if I was onto something good and whether I should continue writing the series. But you, my incredible readers, showed me the light. You've not just encouraged me to keep spinning this tale, but you've helped me find a deep, passionate love for storytelling, especially stories that pack a punch with their messages. I'm touched by how many of you connected with these pages' deeper meanings and lessons.

I have been trying to write this series for years, but something always got in the way: lack of confidence, work, and other priorities. I thought the urge to write would go away after a while, but the story haunted me, and I had to get it out there, at least out of my head. However, because of you, I am now a full-time author, making a good living from my books, and I've only been doing it for three years.

So this might be the end of this series, but don't worry, David, Jessica, and our magical Scottish crew aren't going anywhere. There's a lot more to come in this magical universe!

Thank you for sticking with me and making this journey unforgettable. I now get to do something I love and earn a full-time income.

Here's to lots more magickal adventures together! 🧙 ✨ 📚

CHAPTER 1

As Jacqueline raised her hand, tracing a mystical sigil in the air, she chanted the incantation with increasing fervour. Sensing the gathering power, Alicia instinctively stepped back, her energies coiling to prepare for a potential clash.

It all happened in a split second. Alicia looked at the others in the room, who could only stand and watch, having no time to react.

Jacqueline's voice grew stronger as she continued to chant the incantation. Her resolve was firm as she focused on Alicia.

The room was lit up with a bright orange glow. Everyone shielded their eyes except for Jacqueline, who chanted in the centre of the room.

Alicia had been caught off guard, but now, she unshielded her eyes and looked defiantly at Jacqueline as if challenging her. She had shielded herself before projecting to Genevieve's house, but she hadn't expected anybody to attack her. As she was about to retaliate with her magick, she felt something strange happening, and it took a moment for her to realise that the temperature inside her shield was rising unnaturally fast.

Jacqueline continued with her magick, but she was faltering. Her voice was a little weaker and a little less authoritative now.

Alicia smiled, knowing that Jacqueline's power was waning. But something was happening to her shield. Its strength was wavering, and the heat inside Alicia's cocoon of protection was still rising rapidly. Alicia realised what Jacqueline was doing. The high temperature inside her protective zone could not hold, and Alicia would be powerless and temporarily disarmed of any magick, giving Jacqueline time to bind, harm, or even kill her.

Alicia calmly closed her eyes and recited her incantations. She focused hard to the exclusion of everything that was going on around her. The temperature inside her protective zone dropped a little. She opened her eyes and watched as Jacqueline stood, arms now outstretched and sweat rolling down her forehead. She looked at Alicia, eyes wide, as the realisation dawned on her that she had figured out her plan.

Jacqueline now tried harder, exerted more energy, and shouted louder. She forced it, and it was clear it was a last-gasp effort to make her spell work. She was now running on empty.

Alicia smiled at Jacqueline and looked at the others in the room, who watched in shock at what Jacqueline was doing. It was clear to Alicia that Genevieve, Jonathan, and possibly even Logan did not know what Jacqueline had planned when Alicia had ported over to Genevieve's.

Jacqueline slowly lowered her hands and slumped a little as she looked at Alicia. Logan came rushing over and stood in front of her as if protecting her from what Alicia might do.

Alicia surprised herself as she calmly and slowly walked over to Logan and Jacqueline.

"Tell me," she said, looking directly at Jacqueline. "Were you trying to bind my magick, or were you trying to kill me?"

Jacqueline, with her head slumped in exhaustion, lifted her head slightly and looked directly into Alicia's eyes, "I was trying to kill you." Genevieve gasped in the background, which confirmed to Alicia that she did not know what Jacqueline had planned.

"I thought as much. Your plan obviously backfired, but I have to say it was admirable, and I almost fell for it," Alicia said as she raised her head and, with two fingers, lifted Jacqueline's head further.

Logan grabbed Alicia's arm, "Do not harm her, Alicia. She is trying to protect us, her son, and everyone else. You cannot go through with this crazy plan of yours."

Alicia immediately grabbed Logan's throat, "Get your fucking hand off me now before I rip your throat out."

Just then, Alicia saw Jonathan rushing forward out of the corner of her eye. With a deft flick, she projected an invisible spell that sent Jonathan hurtling through the air. His back slammed against the wall, and his head cracked heavily against the stone. He slumped to the ground, unconscious.

Genevieve shouted at Alicia, "Stop," as she rushed over to Jonathan and cradled his head.

Genevieve turned around to Alicia, "You have to stop this now," she shouted, turning back around to tend to Jonathan.

Alicia, still gripping Logan's throat, with Jacqueline weakly trying to prise Alicia's hand from her husband's throat. "You dared to lure me into a trap to kill me, and now you don't want to pay the consequences of that action." She gripped tighter on Logan's throat.

Logan could only grab at Alicia's wrist. He, too, was losing consciousness as he gasped for air.

"No, no, stop this. It was my idea. I didn't talk to anyone about this," Jacqueline shouted, still trying to take Alicia's hand off Logan's throat. "I swear, nobody else knew what I would do."

Alicia looked at her and admired Jacqueline's

tenacity and courage for a split second, but she couldn't let that happen without some form of retribution.

Jacqueline looked at Alicia pleadingly, willing her to let go of her grip on Logan's throat, who was close to losing consciousness.

Alicia thought for a second before letting go of Logan. He immediately dropped to the ground onto his knees and gasped for air.

Alicia stared at Jacqueline with fury and burning in her eyes. A fire raged inside her now, and she needed to enact retribution.

Then, without warning, Jacqueline watched the fire inside Alicia fizzle out. She squirmed as Alicia stood smiling at her, who was now calm and in complete control. She looked at Jacqueline and then at Genevieve, who was still tending to Jonathan. "I know just how to harm you without touching you."

Jacqueline looked at her and narrowed her eyes, questioning.

"Send my regards to David. Oh, wait, perhaps that won't be possible."

At this, Alicia quickly opened a portal and walked through it, looking back at the group before stepping into it.

CHAPTER 2

"**K**eep going higher. You can do it. Raise your energy to another frequency," the woman said as she watched David, Jessica, and ten other students. They were in a forest clearing with freezing cold water holes in the ground and had been training for one hour per night over several days.

On the seventh evening of their intensive regimen, following a day of rigorous exercises, they delved into training designed to tune out external distractions and hone in on their internal energy frequencies. They aimed to elevate these frequencies across multiple levels, enhancing their mastery and control.

In front of them were large glass tubes that lit up as they reached a different energy frequency. They would change colour as they passed through several layers of energy frequencies.

After around ten minutes, several students jumped

out of their waterholes, reaching a yellow or green colour on the glass tube. They were happy with their progress and watched the others silently as they dried and heated themselves with warm towels.

The female trainer in the white robe walked around the water holes. Now, with five students left out of the original twelve. They had been in there for fifteen minutes now.

David kept his eyes gently closed as he tried to block out what was happening outside his body. It was a strange feeling; he could feel the cold on his skin, but after ten minutes in the water hole, it felt like his mind had drifted out of his body without astral projection. He knew instinctively when he had reached another energy frequency in his body, as he felt a clicking whenever he levelled up to another frequency. In the first ten minutes, he briefly opened his eyes to check the colours on the glass tube before him. He now kept his eyes closed and sensed the colours. He was feeling the vibration of the colours from the glass tube.

He now sensed Jessica, three holes to his left. He sensed the trainer's presence nearby, perceiving her satisfaction with the student's progress in their learning.

He focused his mind on a light travelling up through his body from the base of his spine.

"David?" Jessica whispered.

David felt a little shocked when he heard Jessica whispering to him. How was this possible? The rules

forbade them from astral projecting during this training, David thought to himself.

"I can sense you, David, but I'm not projecting. I
think I've switched to the same frequency as you. Talk
to me and see if it works." Jessica said.

"Can you hear me if I think of something?" David
said, testing his communication with Jessica.

"Yes, it's working. I can hear you. Don't get too
excited, though. You'll lose the frequency level you're
on," Jessica said.

"Jeezus, this is on another level," David said.

"Literally," Jessica replied, laughing.

David laughed in his mind.

"Okay, we have to focus here. I just wanted to touch
base," Jessica said. David felt her presence leaving him.

David focused on raising the light through his body
and lifting it through the crown of his head. A beautiful
white light gave him energy throughout his whole body.
The white light would oscillate, and he could almost
feel a subtle vibration in his body as he tingled.

Another light shone outside his body now. It was
bright blue, so bright he thought he had opened his
eyes for a second. He tightened his eyes to make sure
they were still closed. He thought his perception of the
energy frequencies must be stronger if he could now
see the colours without opening his eyes.

He could feel his body in the cold water and was
still aware of his surroundings, knowing he was in the
forest. He saw the female instructor in her white robe

looking down on him. Am I astral projecting? he wondered. It didn't feel as if he was outside his body. He didn't feel the usual heaviness of his astral self; this felt entirely different.

He looked again at the instructor and the other students as they looked down on him and Jessica. All the holes in the ground were empty except for himself and Jessica's.

The lights on their glass tubes were now glowing violet and lit up the forest area.

He could hear the instructor laughing. He heard her speaking. "They have transcended. They are now operating between the space of the physical realm and the astral realm."

What does that even mean? He asked himself.

"How amazing is this," Jessica whispered. He could feel her presence but could not see her.

"I don't even know what this is. How can we exist between the physical and the astral?" He asked.

Just then, he felt another presence beside them. It was the instructor.

"Okay, David and Jessica, it's time to return to the physical. Well done to both of you; what you have done is impressive. Now come on back."

David thought about his physical body again and tried to feel the coldness of the water. It was coming through; he could feel the cold against his skin.

He slowly opened his eyes and looked up at the crowd of students looking down on him and Jessica.

The students started cheering when both were fully back in their bodies and aware. David stole a look at Jessica, and they smiled.

With warm towels wrapped around them, David and Jessica dried themselves off fully while speaking to the other students about their experience of transcendence.

David didn't think what he did was a big deal, but to the other students, it was. He had noticed his ego was less in control these days, and he was no longer impressed or in awe of the lessons he had been learning daily.

Jessica seemed to feel the same way. Although they marvelled at the world of energy, it was more of a feeling of coming home and re-learning than learning something for the first time.

As the other students drifted off in front of them, the instructor held back to speak to the two of them.

"The skill and courage you both exhibited are far from ordinary; take pride in your remarkable feat. However, accolades are not your path, and you are both far down the line on your journey of transcendence." She said, lifting her robe from the stony path that led back to the castle.

Jessica looked at the instructor and took a deep breath. "We've been here for over one year now, and it feels like we're only just starting our journey," she said, and David nodded in agreement.

The instructor smiled, "That is a great attitude to

have. We never stop learning, and we never will, no matter how much we learn. A healer learns to heal after years of training but still discovers new things even after twenty or thirty years of being a healer. I have taught energy systems for over thirty years, and my students, like you two, are still teaching me new things every day," the instructor said, smiling.

"So, will we ever know enough to be competent magick practitioners?" David asked.

The instructor sighed as she pulled back her long dark hair from the sides of her face and tied it into a knot at the back of her head, "You find that 20 per cent of what you have and will learn at the academy will account for 80 per cent of what you use daily."

She then stopped walking.

David and Jessica stopped and turned to look at her.

"You two have already learned enough to be exceptional practitioners of magick, and there is still so much potential in you. I need you to know that. We rarely lavish praise at the academy, yet you both must realise how exceptional you truly are. Be prepared for the exciting journey ahead," the instructor said, continuing to walk along the path.

David and Jessica looked at each other and smiled.

David ambled along, lost in his thoughts. Just as they reached the castle gates, he said, "Wait, what do you mean, 'Be prepared for the exciting journey ahead'?"

Jessica looked at him and then at the instructor.

The instructor stopped and smiled at the two of them. Without answering, she turned and walked along the corridor to the instructor's rooms.

Jessica turned to David, "I guess she's not telling us what she meant. Do you fancy spending some time with me in the lounge area? There probably won't be anybody there just now."

"Oh! You want to get me alone, do you? Are you trying to have your wicked way with me?" David said, laughing.

Jessica tutted and rolled her eyes, "You're not that lucky. No, I want to take a few hours off studying."

Yeah, I think we've done enough studying and learning for the day," David said as he motioned for Jessica to go first.

"Can I ask you something, Jess?" David said as he followed her.

"Uh, oh!" Jessica replied, smiling at him.

"No, it's nothing bad or serious or anything. I just wanted to know if you still have sexual thoughts about us. You know, it seems like a while ago now, and we never really did anything after it despite how amazing it was," David asked her.

"Who said it was amazing?" she said, laughing as she walked along.

David pushed her from behind, "Well, it was for me, you cheeky git." he said.

Jessica stopped walking. She grabbed the towel that was wrapped around his neck, pulled him into her and kissed him hard. "It was for me too, but we're here to learn about being witches, and you and your sexy arse are a distraction. But, yes, I still have sexual thoughts about you."

She placed her hand on his cheek, smiled and continued walking toward the lounge.

David smiled to himself, held his shoulders back a little more, stood up a little taller and continued to follow her.

CHAPTER 3

Genevieve cradled the cup of tea as she stared off into space.

She heard the living room door creaking and turned around to see her sister Jacqueline.

Sleep had left her hair in a tangled mess. "What are you doing up, it's five o'clock in the morning?" She said, looking at Genevieve in surprise.

"I could ask you the same question, but I suspect we're both still worried about what Alicia said the other day when she was here," Genevieve replied as she stood up. "Fancy a cuppa?"

"Yes, that would be lovely." Jacqueline followed her older sister through to the kitchen.

A steaming pot of tea was already on a thick wooden tray on the counter. Genevieve poured a cup of tea and handed it to Jacqueline to add milk.

"How is Jonathan doing?"

"Ach! He's a tough one. He was much better before going to sleep last night. Helen was over yesterday again to look over him." Genevieve said.

"She seems to be a talented healer," Jacqueline said, sipping her tea.

"Yes, we've known her for years. She's great. We have a great bond with her. She's younger than most healers, but she knows her stuff. She's well-versed in Dream Dancing, too, so she knows some problems that can arise from astral projecting," Genevieve said.

Jacqueline pursed her lips together and looked apologetically at Genevieve. "Gen, I am sorry. I didn't mean for Jonathan to get hurt or to mix you up in this. I just thought..."

"Jac, it's fine. I was angry initially, but I completely understand why you did it. If anything, it highlights the need to take action. I just wouldn't have done it the way you did it." Genevieve said, smiling at her affectionately.

Jacqueline had always been one to take risks without thinking about the consequences. Genevieve remembered when they had both been astral projecting to houses in their street to spy on their neighbours. One night, they had discovered a drug den where the occupants had thousands of bags of MDMA. They were dealers. They had both witnessed their neighbour coming to the door to buy a bag. The girl was a friend of Jacqueline's, and she was only fourteen years old. Jacqueline was furious.

They had both planned to go back to the neighbour's house and port into it and flush all the drugs down the toilet. Genevieve wanted to tell their parents so they could call the police anonymously. However, Jacqueline had other plans. She wanted to cut off the source of the drugs. For nine days, they followed their drug-dealing neighbours and eventually came to an old warehouse where they were manufacturing the MDMA. Jacqueline was beside herself with excitement.

The following night, they both projected to the warehouse. They didn't think anybody would be in it at night. When they projected, there was a hive of activity with men and women milling around inside the warehouse and many cars coming and going outside. Genevieve suggested getting back to their own home and doing this another time. Instead, Jacqueline physically ported into the warehouse without telling Genevieve of her plans and tipped some of the Bunsen burners onto the nearby chemical stores. The fire had spread rapidly, and several explosions ensued. Some of the drug makers had seen Jacqueline and had run to grab her. Genevieve quickly ported into the warehouse and threw barrels before Jacqueline's pursuers. When Jacqueline spotted what was happening, they both projected back to their own home. Genevieve had been furious with her younger sister for weeks.

Things had changed little since then, and even though Genevieve was eight years older than her sister, she still looked up to her and admired her courage and bravery.

"What do we do now? Do you think she'll be able to get to David at the Academy?" Jacqueline asked.

"Alicia is powerful, and I suspect we don't know half her power, so I suspect she will get to David. I have contacted Joseph, who assures me she shouldn't be able to get by their defences, but he will contact the academy heads to warn them of any impending danger." Genevieve said.

"I've been digging with Logan, and we don't feel she will carry through with what she said. I think she's got more important things to worry about." Jacqueline said, smirking.

Genevieve held up her hand. "I don't even want to know what you've found out. We've got enough to worry about."

Jacqueline smiled and took another sip of her tea. "It's been twenty-two days since David and Jessica have been at the academy. They should finish up soon."

"Another half a year in their time. They must have learned a hell of a lot by now. I think they'll both come out of the academy different people and more powerful witches." Genevieve said. She looked at her sister again. "Do you regret leaving David with me all those years ago?"

Jacqueline looked at Genevieve and took a deep breath. "Do you know, Gen? We had many conversations about coming back and living an ordinary life, well, as ordinary a life as you can be being a witch. We have made the world a better place for what we did without endangering our son. And you have done an amazing job with him."

Genevieve smiled. "He's been challenging, and he always asked about you both, but he's turned out to be an amazing young man, and it seems he's going to be an exceptional witch too."

They both turned as the living room door creaked again.

Jonathan rubbed the sleep out of his eyes. "What are you two doing up? It's five thirty in the morning?"

Genevieve and Jacqueline looked at each other and laughed.

CHAPTER 4

H er plan to destroy the Akashic records was getting closer. Alicia paced around her New York apartment, thinking about the next step of her plan.

She'd already figured out the magick she would need to destroy the Akashic records, but the next part of the plan was much trickier: How did she put a better version of the records in place? It wasn't like a computer program that she could upgrade.

She knew Saad, her team and Jacqueline Gordon, Genevieve's sister, were right. The world would spiral out of control without a hook to hang their thousands of years of memories, ideas, symbols, and archetypes, and the collective consciousness would be without its database from which to download. She'd thought about that for years.

She had been planning this and believed she had

found a way of effectively upgrading the software. The only problem was that her theory was untestable; it was a one-time try, a success or a failure, with no in-between.

Now that she was close to implementing her ambitious plan, she doubted herself. What would be the worst that would happen? She had figured the worst that could happen was that everyone would lose access to collective consciousness, which would cause chaos throughout the world. She imagined people not having a religion, not having a sense of right from wrong, and being unable to decipher who they were and what they stood for. Everyone would lose their sense of identity, literally, not just metaphorically.

She imagined it being like a zombie apocalypse, where eight billion people around the world would be alive but just wandering about aimlessly. Then the killing would start, and survival of the fittest would kick in. The reptilian brain would take over, and people would start killing other people to survive. Would the NeoCortex of the brain still function, she wondered. As a powerful witch, she had always been interested in the psychology of human beings, and she had learned long ago about the triune brain theory: Neo-Cortex for speech, logic and higher thinking; the limbic system for emotions; and the reptilian brain for instinct and survival.

Could she be so cruel as to throw eight billion people into a turmoil like this if it all went wrong? If she couldn't install a new database or overwrite parts of the current database, which is the collective consciousness, this was effectively what she was doing to the world.

She suddenly realised for the first time that she had the power to destroy humanity as she knew it.

A surge of energy erupted inside her, spreading throughout her whole body and beyond. A lightness and an energy she had never felt infused her etheric body. Her physical body found it hard to breathe. It felt almost like a panic attack, which she'd had as a child after what had happened to her. Only this was more like an excited panic attack. It was like she was being fed energy from a different source. She went with the flow to see where this would take her.

Her mind opened to something higher, something she had never felt, something much more powerful than she'd ever felt.

Alicia felt a compulsion to retreat to the pentacle that lay underneath the large rug on her living room floor. She folded some of the fifteen-foot rug to get a good grip, then dragged the carpet with the coffee table on top to reveal the beautiful pentacle.

She marvelled again at the intricate design of it. The five points had been meticulously etched with an intricate design, blending ancient runes and symbols of the natural elements: earth, air, fire, water, and spirit. These symbols were not just decorative; they served as conduits for channelling energy, their precision amplifying the pentacle's power.

She slowly took off her clothes and laid them on the couch.

Now naked, she stepped inside the circle and felt another surge of energy enter her.

Alicia mentally closed the circle in her mind with a short incantation to protect her from outside forces.

She gently lay down in the middle of the pentacle and spread her arms wide, still feeling the energy pouring into her. It was exhilarating, and her whole body tingled.

All the while, she wondered where this energy was coming from.

She was a witch and was used to different energy types flowing through her, but this differed from anything else she had felt.

She closed her eyes and surfed on the wave of energy that she felt flowing through her and all around her. Her stomach felt twisted and in knots, but it was a pleasurably painful experience. She convulsed with the pleasure, baulked at the pain, and felt her mind drifting to another dimension.

Her body arched in the middle of the pentacle, her long dark hair cascading around the north point. She writhed and moaned as waves of energy flowed through her.

Her body then became utterly rigid. Alicia opened her eyes and wondered what was happening. She wasn't afraid, more curious. She closed her eyes again as another surge overcame her. Her body then slowly rose in the air. She let her arms drop to her sides, and her legs went limp. Some unseen force had now taken hold of her. Was another entity entering her? What was this fresh energy she was feeling? Was it male or female? She didn't feel it was nefarious. Lots of questions were swirling around her mind as she hung in midair, energy surging through her.

After a few minutes of floating in mid-air and the pleasurable pain of the energy flowing through her, she drifted back down to the ground.

As her body touched the ground and she was lying flat on her back, the energy withdrew from her body as she opened her eyes.

As she sat up, five women were standing on each of the points of the star. She recognised them as being different versions of herself. They all looked very similar to her, yet each woman was distinctively different.

"What the..." She whispered aloud as she looked at each of the women. They all smiled affectionately at her as if they were long-lost friends.

One of them stepped forward and held her hand out to help Alicia stand up. Out of curiosity, Alicia took the woman's hand to see whether she was a physical being. She was physical. The woman pulled Alicia gently to her feet, looked at her lovingly and then wrapped her arms around her. She squeezed her tightly. Alicia could only stand there. She was determined to see where this led and just went with what the woman wanted to do.

The woman kept squeezing Alicia tighter and tighter, and then there she felt a popping sensation in her body as if the woman had squeezed herself into Alicia's body. For a few seconds, she couldn't figure out what the hell happened, but then Alicia felt another surge, and she immediately understood that the woman had infused her energy with Alicia's. This happened with the other four versions of herself.

After an hour sitting on her couch, Alicia still contemplated what had happened. She'd never heard of anything like this happening from any witch, and she knew a lot of powerful witches.

She thought about everyone she knew and who she could contact to ask about this. She decided on a dear friend, Dana, whom she'd never spoken to in a few years.

As she prepared herself a cappuccino, she pushed the button on her phone to call Dana.

After exchanging pleasantries, Alicia got down to what she wanted to know.

"Listen, I've just had a strange experience, and you're the only one I can think of who would know anything about it," Alicia said, sipping her cappuccino.

"Oh, I like the sound of this. What's happened?" Dana said in her Irish lilt.

Alicia explained precisely what had happened to her, from the energy surge to the five women entering

THE WITCHES OF SCOTLAND | 25

her and giving her more energy. Even in the presence of another witch, voicing it made Alicia feel somewhat foolish; the words seemed absurd.

There was a pause after Alicia had described what had happened.

"Are you still there?" Alicia asked as the silence continued longer than expected.

"Yes...yes, I'm still here." Dana said, a little less cheerily than she had been a few minutes earlier.

Alicia waited a few more seconds. "Well, is it bad, good or?"

Dana interrupted her, "What are you planning, Alicia?"

"What! What do you mean?" Alicia replied.

"What you've just experienced is called The Coalescing. Alicia, it doesn't normally happen unless you need huge resources. I can't think of anything requiring this amount of resources at your fingertips." Dana said, sounding a little worried and curious at the same time.

Alicia sat up and was a little more alert now. "When has it happened in the past? You know about this, so when has it happened to other witches?"

Dana hesitated again, "There's only been a few times I know, but I'm sure there are other times in history..."

"Why are you being so vague, Dana? What is it? Just tell me straight," Alicia said, not understanding, as

Dana was usually so forthright, which is one quality Alicia admired in her.

"Coalescing happens when there is going to be a tremendous shift in the collective consciousness. The five sisters appear when you require an enormous amount of universal energy derived from Earth, air, fire, water, and spirit—essentially, a lot of power from the universe. You should feel blessed, but the question is, what are you planning for the universe to give you this much power?" Dana asked.

Alicia fell silent. This is a sign that what I am planning is the right thing to do, she thought. I must be on the right path.

"Alicia? You okay?" Dana asked.

Alicia looked at the phone in her hand, pressed the red button and hung up on Dana. Now lost in a cloud of emotions, questions, ideas, thoughts, excitement and energy. Five sisters, The Coalescing, a tremendous shift in the collective consciousness. She thought about what Dana had told her.

She steeled herself and stood up from the couch. "I'm on the right path," she whispered to herself and then said louder.

CHAPTER 5

David and Jessica had passed another monthly test, and there were only a few more to go before the final one. The final monthly test was a battle where the top witches at the academy would take all the lessons they had learned over the last two years and battle with each other.

Jessica was looking forward to it but didn't see the point of doing a battle as such. She knew she was good and didn't need to prove it in battle. She could see the benefit of it as it showed what the witches could do in a stressful situation.

Talking to David, Jessica knew David felt the same way as her, which was unlike him as he was usually very competitive.

They had been getting on great over the last few months, and although the sexual tension was still there, they had both held off, focusing on their intensive studying and practice.

It seemed the way she looked at the world had changed entirely, and she felt confident that she didn't need to view it in the same way. Her perceptions had changed altogether, and she felt good.

Sitting at the edge of her bed reading, waiting to enter another learning room, she read some of her favourite texts. It was an old book, not from witchcraft but from an author called Neville Goddard, and once considered a religious text, it was now seen as a book to learn about universal energy. When rereading the book, it was clear that Neville had indeed harnessed the universal energy power that many witches spoke about. She had read other books from the 'New Thought' leaders of old from the eighteen hundreds and the nineteen hundreds. Many of them had touched their inner power and were teaching so as not to offend the religious leaders of the time.

A chiming sound rang out as a blue light turned on, signalling to Jessica that she had one minute before the doors to the learning room opened.

"What do we have in store today, Shallan?" She asked the AI assistant.

"I think you will like this one today, Jessica. You will meet with someone you admire and learn more about universal energy." The voice replied.

"Oh, that sounds good. Anybody famous?" Jessica said as she packed a bottle of water into her rucksack.

"Yes, it's Neville Goddard." the voice said as the door opened to the learning room.

Jessica looked up in surprise and delight. She loved this way of learning and would miss it when she left.

The doors slid open, and Jessica walked into the streets of nineteen-fifties New York.

She looked around in awe, recognising the feel of the place and almost familiar streets from watching old movies depicting New York in the fifties. Jessica recalled a scene from Godfather in which Robert DeNiro was first starting his empire. She remembered DeNiro walking along the rooftops, looking down at a funeral procession. Where she was walking now looked like this scene. Crowds of people rushing to and from work filled the streets. There were street artists on the corner, a hot dog vendor with his cart shouting "hot dogs", newspaper boys shouting the day's headlines, shoe shiners, and flower sellers who added splashes of colour to the urban grey with their carts full of fresh flowers.

Jessica wandered around the streets and didn't even think about who she was there to meet. She was in a happy daze. There was poverty here but also a sense of camaraderie among the people. A lot of the men would have just come back from fighting in World War 2. *Maybe I am romanticising this,* she thought as she paid more attention to what was happening around her.

As she walked, she looked up to see a huge marble arch. She stopped walking and stared up at it.

"Impressive, isn't it?" Someone from behind her said.

Jessica spun around. She recognised Neville Goddard immediately from the photographs she had seen online.

He held out his hand. "I am Neville Goddard. And you must be Jessica Campbell?"

He had a warm aura about him and a protective, father-figure demeanour. "Yes, I am. It's amazing to meet you. I've read a lot of your work."

He blushed slightly and bowed his head.

Jessica smiled and turned back around to the arch. "It is impressive, awe-inspiring." She walked to her right to get a better look at George Washington's monuments.

Neville said, "They added the sculptures of George Washington to the original arch about twenty years after its construction."

Jessica had a stare on and forced herself out of it to acknowledge this great man standing next to her. She turned around and looked at his tanned face. His eyes had a look of mischievousness in them.

He smiled warmly and motioned for them to walk underneath the arch.

"You're learning a lot about universal energy, I gather," He said as they strolled toward the fountain.

His voice had a soothing effect on Jessica, and she felt at ease in his company. His brown pinstripe suit would look fashionable by today's standards. She looked up at him, "I have learned a lot over the two years, well three and a bit weeks earth time, but nearly two years on this level..." she fumbled with her words, trying to explain the differences between the different levels.

He laughed, gently chiding her, "I know how time works on different levels, so it's okay."

Jessica was relieved. She was with a man whose works she admired and was making a fool of herself.

"What lessons have you taken from my books?" He asked

Now he was putting her on the spot, she thought. She relaxed and mentally reviewed some of her favourite books. "Well, I have to be honest and say that all the religious stuff in the books is not for me, but what I did was replace the word God with life force, and it made much more sense when I read it like this."

He laughed, "Well, you write what you have to get through to the masses, and religion in the 1950s was big."

Jessica nodded, "Oh, I totally get that, and I suspected you were deeply religious, but your writing had so much more depth to it, and people who got it just...got it."

"That's very perceptive of you. And what did you think about when I wrote about feelings being an integral part of having a life you desire?" He asked, looking down at her.

"Well, that's the part I am now beginning to understand, having gone through the training that I've had.

Feelings bring about a different level of energy within us, and we are effectively operating at a different level from what we are used to. Without directing our feelings and beliefs, I think you wrote we live on an average level of energy. However, we can escape that and effectively design a life we want."

He nodded as they continued to walk. Once they reached the water fountain, he invited her to sit on the bench.

As they sat, Jessica continued, "So the more I learn, the more I see the subtext of what you're talking about in your books and your lectures. It's quite enlightening. It's almost as if you wrote the books to speak to different people depending on where they are in their understanding of universal energy."

"Well, I have to say, few people have understood my books to such a depth as you, but you're right. I wrote books for beginners, intermediates and advanced life practitioners. We all have different levels of understanding on which we operate; some of us stay at the lower levels all our lives, others strive to reach the higher planes, and you have reached the higher planes. But there's still much more to learn." He sat with his elbows on his knees and took out a pipe from his pocket. He patted some of the tobacco in the pipe's bowl and then lit a match to light it.

Jessica watched him, thinking this was all surreal, but she was getting used to doing surreal.

As he blew out a puff of smoke from his mouth, he

turned to Jessica and motioned his head toward the cloud of smoke he had just exhaled, "That smoke cloud is just like our thoughts. It's aimless and just spreads around and eventually disappears." He took another puff on his pipe and inhaled the smoke and, this time, exhaled as if he was whistling. This time, the smoke went up in a straight line before eventually dispersing. "That is like directed thoughts, we will get to where we want to go much quicker with directed thoughts, and the energy we require will help us gather momentum and get there quicker than we thought possible. Most people will never get that. That is why it is important to direct our thoughts on where we want to go and not focus on what we don't want, which is the problem. Most people are just thinking thoughts like clouds of aimless smoke."

Jessica thought about this for a few seconds. "The problem is we're not taught to direct our thoughts. The teachings you offer once dismissed as 'woo woo,' are now gaining recognition for their significance. However, primarily those beyond the mainstream embrace and impart this knowledge. There's a palpable shift towards appreciating and valuing the insights you provide."

"That's good to hear. This will take a long time to become mainstream until science proves it. We have hung our hats and jackets on the coat hooks of religion for so long it's going to be hard to break the cycle. However, that's where you come in," he said, looking at Jessica while taking another puff of his pipe.

"What do you mean?" She asked.

"You're going to help to teach, little by little, until there's huge momentum and quantifiable evidence to prove what you're talking about. That's the purpose of the Witches of Scotland." Neville said, looking out toward 5th Avenue.

Jessica shook her head. "If I ever shared what I've learned over the years, people would laugh at me and ridicule me because I'm a witch."

"People believe what they see, Jessica, not what they are told," he replied, looking at her.

"Meaning?" Jessica retorted, hoping he didn't mean showing the world her porting from one place to another.

"You know what I mean. You'll be ridiculed, then revered, then accepted," he said as he tapped out the tobacco remains in his pipe and put it in his pocket.

"I'm not sure I want that responsibility," Jessica said, thinking about the implications of showing her true self to the world.

Neville smiled sympathetically, "You were born a witch, Jessica. You have been granted powers beyond a human's and must take responsibility for them. Do you think I had a choice when I was given the ability to access the Akashic records?"

Jessica stared ahead to Fifth Avenue and pondered what Neville was saying.

"So, what would happen if the Akashic records were

destroyed?" Jessica asked, thinking about what she was really at the academy for.

Neville looked at her and then turned his attention back to his pipe. He took it out of his pocket and tapped it against the side of the bench. He then repacked it with tobacco before relighting it.

"Well, Jessica, I didn't believe that could ever happen."

"But, I take it, you know different now?" Jessica asked.

"Yes. Yes, I do, and it would be a tragedy, but you are here to stop that, aren't you? So we should all be safe." Neville said with a slight smirk.

Jessica couldn't tell if he believed that or if he was just gently teasing her again.

They continued to speak for a few hours, visiting different places in the area whilst Neville taught her more about energy, personal energy and universal energy.

Jessica felt elated when she got back to her room.

CHAPTER 6

David spoke briefly with his AI assistant about today's lessons and hurried from his room into a new setting. It was a forest area. No one was there to greet him as there had been the other times.

David looked around and just saw lots and lots of trees. He wandered, not worried, but would wait to see what happened.

As he walked through the thick forest undergrowth, he came to a barely visible path.

Looking around and feeling relaxed, David followed the path to find where it led. As he ambled through the forest, taking in the sounds, smells and feel of the forest, he noticed someone sitting on an enormous tree trunk. The trunk's roots were still showing as it had toppled over.

He could make out more of the man sitting down as

he got closer. His silver-grey hair was the first thing that stood out to David. He wore a loose-fitting white cheesecloth shirt, khaki-coloured baggy linen trousers, and sandals. The man looked up and held up his hand.

David smiled and walked toward him.

"David, very nice to meet you," he said as he held out his hand. He had an accent hailing from London but not a cockney accent.

David shook the stranger's hand, "Erm, nice to meet you too."

"Ah, you don't know who I am. My name is Stuart Wilde. I was a metaphysical teacher when I was alive." He said, smiling.

David had heard the name before and struggled through his memory banks to find where it originated. "Stuart Wilde, I know the name but can't quite..." Then David stopped and, with eyes wide, "Oh! Stuart Wilde, the author of 'Infinite Self' and other books." He struggled to recall the other books he had read.

"The one and only," he said, sitting back on the tree trunk.

"Are you here to teach me something then?" David asked.

He chuckled and said, "Well, I hope so, mate; otherwise, this trip would be a waste for both of us."

"Are you..." David tried to think of a tactful way to put it: "Still with us on the earth plane."

Stuart laughed, "No, I have not been on the Earth

plane for about fourteen years. My physical body ceased to be in 2013."

"Oh, I didn't realise you had passed." David said, thinking he should say something like 'I'm sorry to hear that', but he didn't feel it was right.

Stuart sensed that David felt a little awkward in this situation. "Not to worry, my friend. We don't die, as I wrote in my books; we just move our consciousness somewhere else. Right now, I am here with you, and hopefully, I will teach you something that you can use in your life."

"So you're part of the collective consciousness then?" David asked, settling into the trunk of the tree a little more.

"Oh, we are all part of the collective, son. The tick-tock world you live in even contributes to the collective."

"Tick-tock world?" David asked.

Stuart looked into David's eyes, "The tick-tock world. It's a term I use to describe the mechanical, almost robotic life that society traps us into. It's all about the relentless march of time—tick-tock, tick-tock—where everyone's rushing from one place to another, chasing after material success without ever asking, "Why?"

David pondered this for a few seconds, "So, it's about being caught up in the rat race?"

Stuart sat upright and held out his arms, "Exactly. It's

a world where people live by the clock, governed by schedules, deadlines, and an endless list of societal expectations. It's a place where people are so focused on doing what they're 'supposed to do' that they forget to live, explore, and be. They lose touch with the magick of existence, the spontaneity of life, and their infinite selves."

David nodded, understanding Stuart's question: "How do we stop living in the tick-tock world?"

Stuart was in full flow now, "Oh, It's not about physically escaping; it's about shifting your perception, about seeing through the illusion of the material world and recognising that there's so much more to existence. Start by questioning the norms, the shoulds and musts. Why are you doing the things you do? Are they bringing you joy, fulfilment, and spiritual growth? You've got to keep asking questions every day; don't accept what society tells you to accept."

David again nodded in agreement with Stuart, caught up in his energy and enthusiasm. "And what about time? How do we deal with that in the non-tick-tock world?"

Stuart nodded as if he had expected this question. "Time is a construct, my friend. Yes, we live in a world where time is a reality, but how we experience it is up to us. In the tick-tock world, time is a tyrant. Outside of it, time is a flow, a rhythm you dance to in harmony with the universe. It's about being present, living fully in the moment, and aligning yourself with the natural cycles of life rather than the artificial pace of the modern world."

David listened intently, puffed out his cheeks and raised his eyebrows, "It sounds liberating but a little difficult to achieve in this world."

"Liberation often comes through challenge. It's a journey of awakening, of seeing the world and yourself in a new light. Start small. Meditate. Spend time in nature. Listen to your inner voice. Gradually, you'll step out of the tick-tock into a reality where life is richer, deeper, and infinitely more fulfilling. Remember, the key to freedom lies within you." Stuart Said.

He stopped to look at David, letting him digest what he was saying.

David stood up, "So..." he couldn't think of another question to ask now. He sensed a glimpse of understanding had been granted to him, yet he struggled to think of the right questions to explore it further.

Having seen this reaction before, Stuart laughed, "Let me ask you something, David. What do you do on the Earth plane?"

David looked at him, "I was a student studying law."

"Excellent and very noble that would have been too. Why did you stop going to university?" Stuart asked him.

"How did you know..." David asked

"I know it all, son," he smiled, warmly waiting for David to answer.

"Well, I...I wasn't doing it for me. I was doing it for my Aunt Gen and wasn't enjoying it." David replied.

"You weren't enjoying it. You were doing it for someone else. That's the same story with everyone else in the world. They do things because they think they should do it, because of family loyalty, or through obligation to loved ones, or to support themselves or their family." Stuart replied quickly.

"But we have to do it to survive," David replied.

"No, we don't. You're still surviving. You're here talking to me now. You're alive and kicking, my friend, and you left university after discovering you were a witch. How bloody exciting is that?"

David laughed. He could feel the excitement build up as the realisation of what Stuart was saying grew inside him.

Stuart stood up. "It's a great feeling, isn't it?" he said, obviously feeling David's excitement.

David nodded and started walking back and forth.

"Walking is good for thinking; do it more often," Stuart said. "Here, follow me," Stuart said as he walked deeper into the forest.

A little puzzled, David followed him.

They had been walking for around five minutes before Stuart stopped at a clearing.

David followed him and realised they were at the edge of the cliff. Stuart looked over the cliff and down.

David, with a mix of curiosity and caution, slowly walked up beside Stuart. He carefully leaned forward to peek over the edge, his heart racing with fear and wonder. As he looked down, he was met with a breathtaking sight. Hundreds of feet below them, the forest canopy spread out in an endless expanse of vibrant green. Sunlight danced through the leaves, casting a kaleidoscope of light and shadow that played across the forest floor far below.

The sheer drop was dizzying, yet there was a mesmerising beauty in the vastness and the sense of untouched wilderness that stretched out before them. It was a moment of pure awe, a reminder of nature's raw power and majesty. David felt a small gasp escape his lips, a spontaneous reaction to the overwhelming spectacle.

Stuart turned to look at David, a knowing smile on his face. "Incredible, isn't it?" he said, his voice barely above a whisper as if to not disturb the sacred stillness of the place.

David could only nod in agreement, his eyes still fixed on the natural marvel before them. For a moment, time seemed to stand still as they stood at the world's edge, enveloped in the serene beauty of the forest and the profound sense of connection to something greater than themselves.

"Now, what would you do if I said jump into the abyss below?" Stuart asked.

David shot him a look, "I'd say you were mad."

Stuart smiled, "Exactly, you'd think about what would happen to you, the fear of jumping, the fear of broken bones, and hurting yourself as you fell through the trees. You just wouldn't do it. But if I didn't ask you that question and instead just pushed you over..."

At this, Stuart grabbed David and jumped over the side of the cliff deep down into the forest below.

CHAPTER 7

They had met a few weeks ago to discuss what was happening. With everything that had happened to Jessica, David, and the Witches of Scotland, Joseph felt he knew what had been happening and, more importantly, why. He heard about the veiled threat to Jacqueline about her son David, but so far, nothing had materialised from that.

Joseph had called Alicia just before Jessica and David had gone to study at the Magick Academy. He didn't know what he hoped to do; he guessed it was just to discover whether the rumours about Alicia destroying the Akashic records were true. To him, it made little sense. Alicia had everything she wanted: power, money, fame, influence, and everything else. She'd had it for years. Why destroy it all now?

He tried to imagine himself in her shoes, but he could not understand why she would risk everything.

She had sounded suspicious about meeting up with him but felt safe enough with him. They had history, and their brief romantic interlude years ago meant she would give him a bit of leeway.

He had cleared his diary and taken a few days off work.

He wasn't used to porting now, as he'd only ported a few times over the last six months. While working on the projects at the Koestler Institute, it was common practice for him to port worldwide. Not so much now that Jessica was helping David discover himself as a witch. Part of him missed it, working with his daughter so closely and part of him, the father's side, was glad she was finding her way and doing something she wanted to do.

He looked in the mirror, straightened his tie, and tucked some hair behind his ears. I *need to get a haircut,* he thought.

He then sat in the brown leather chair in his office, took a deep breath, closed his eyes, and thought about Alicia, her apartment, and her energy. This would be relatively easy, and hopefully, she was waiting for him.

He felt the familiar sensation of his body tingling all over. Joseph knew everyone felt distinct sensations when porting, but he could only describe it as an effervescent tablet being dropped into water. He felt himself dissolving away from his physical body in Edinburgh.

Porting to the other side, in New York, felt different again. Whilst porting out of somewhere felt like his body was dissolving, porting into somewhere felt like his body was being put together quickly, like a fast-motion video of someone building a body made of Lego.

The porting went without a hitch, and Joseph stood in Alicia's living room. She was waiting for him with a smile and two glasses of whiskey.

He smiled, walked over to her, and kissed her on two cheeks while taking a glass from her. "Thank you. This is a pleasant welcome."

Alicia smiled, "Well, as an honoured guest, I think you deserve to be treated well."

Joseph laughed, "Even after everything that's happened?"

"Water under the bridge, Joseph. If I had a daughter, I would have done what you did to me, although you could have just asked me, and I would have told you the truth. You know me, always the truth." Alica said.

Joseph looked at her. Although he still felt very attracted to her, he felt she was being genuine and not playing her business games. The time they had spent together all those years ago still lingered between them, albeit unspoken.

"So, why did you want to talk? What's on your mind?" Alicia asked as she sat at the breakfast bar and rested her elbows on the surface.

Joseph walked over to her and sat opposite her. He sat on the edge of the chair, one foot on the ground and the other on the stool bar. He turned and looked at her and just asked her outright without dancing around the questions,

"Well, number one, are you planning to get David at the Magick Academy? And Number two, are you planning to destroy the Akashic records?"

Alicia raised her eyebrows at this and laughed, a laugh that conveyed that she couldn't quite believe that he had asked her that question. After a few seconds, she looked into his eyes, "Regarding David. No, that was a comment borne out of anger when Jacqueline tried to attack me or rather wanted to kill me."

Joseph sipped his whiskey before replying. "Good. I had an anxious call from Genevieve, worried that you might try to harm David."

"Bigger fish, Joseph," Alicia said, smiling and sipping whiskey from her glass.

Joseph held up his glass to that as if to thank her.

"Regarding your next question," she paused. Yes. Yes, I am planning on destroying the Akashic records. And as long as we're being honest, I have been planning this for years." She looked at Joseph as if challenging him.

"Why? I have tried to think of a hundred reasons you would want to do something like this, but I just can't figure out why you would want to do it. What benefit could you get from doing this?" Joseph asked, genuinely curious.

"Simple. To reset." She replied.

"To reset what? I don't get it?" Joseph replied, leaning forward slightly.

Alicia's face changed from being calm and passive to angry, "The whole fucking world Joseph. You've fucked it up for hundreds of years, and it's culminated in a world where men have taken everything for themselves. Not the ordinary man in the street. I am talking about the men in politics, the men in the industry, the men in the big pharma companies and the men at the top of the education chain. It's all fucked up and has been for centuries, and nobody has come forward to change it. Well, I intend to change it."

Joseph stood up and said, "How do you intend to change it, Alicia? By destroying the minds of eight billion people around the world. How does that change things? You will turn everyone into zombies. What good will your money, power, fame, and fortune do for you once you do that? Surely you have thought about that."

Alicia stood up, "Of course, I have thought about that, and I have a plan."

Joseph turned away, getting angry. "For Christ's sake, Alicia, would you listen to yourself. You sound as if you have a god complex or something trying to save the world from all unscrupulous men in the world. It doesn't work like that. It's human nature for people who want the power to take power, as the people who don't want it don't care. The fact that it's mostly men who want power is why men are the ones who are in control."

Alicia stormed over to Joseph, "You arrogant prick. This is exactly the attitude that got this world into the mess it's in just now. It's mostly men who are in power, as women have always been treated as subservient creatures to men, and if you don't see that, then you're more fucking naïve than I thought, and it gives me all the more reason to reset."

"How the hell are you going to reset the Akashic records? Are you going to destroy them and then put them all back together and mix a little more femininity into the ingredients, and you'll have a gentler version of the Akashic records? Is that it? How the hell are you going to do it, Alicia?" Joseph shouted back, now walking, turning away from her.

"You stupid little man. I can't believe I didn't see this side of you." Alicia said, a little calmer now.

"We see what we want to see, Alicia," Joseph said, turning to her again. "I am not so naïve as to not know that women have been persecuted for hundreds of years. I know that, but it's changing. You surely must see that, too," Joseph said.

Alicia shook her head and laughed, "Tell me, Joseph, when were women allowed to get credit cards?" Joseph looked at her, not knowing, "1980. When were women allowed to have contraception, 1967, and when were they allowed to have mortgages? 1970, when were women allowed to have abortions, 1967 and ridiculously in some states it's being banned again..."

"Okay, okay, I get where..." Joseph said.

Alicia spoke over him and continued, "When was it made illegal to serve a woman in a pub? 1982. When were men legally allowed to rape their wives, Joseph? Legally fuckin' allowed to rape their wives, it was until 1991. Nineteen ninety fuckin' one Joseph, and you're telling me things have changed. Don't be so bloody stupid. Women have always been tolerated, and we're still being tolerated and allowed a little more control from the men who have all the control. If you honestly don't see that, then you're part of the fuckin' problem."

Joseph shook his head as he looked at Alicia.

"Tell me, what percentage of professors in American universities are women?" Alicia asked.

Joseph shook his head, exacerbated. "We could spout statistics all day, Alicia..."

"Thirty-six per cent," Alica said, not waiting for Joseph to finish talking.

He turned to her, "Okay. What percentage of female applicants for professorship roles were women, Alicia? You probably don't know the answer because you're so focused on your biased viewpoint that the number would escape you. Let me tell you the number of female CEOs, the number of female Professors and the number of female politicians, and Females in any other top roles is limited because the number of applicants for those roles is something like five men to one woman, which means statistically, men are more likely to get the role, which means men are being discrimi-nated against for being men as society now feels that there should be more female politicians, CEO's, Professors, etc. So don't come at me for being naïve. I know women have been and still are not being treated fairly, but I am saying it is changing."

Alicia looked at him with rage in her eyes. He could tell she was fuming. He had seen her when she was about to kill a man, and she had that same look now.

CHAPTER 8

After calming down, they agreed to disagree, and Joseph ported back to Edinburgh, still not understanding Alicia's reasons for destroying the Akashic records.

She wondered if he would try to do anything about it before she set her plans. Why wouldn't he, she wondered. She was about to play dice with the entire world; of course, he would try to stop her. If she were in his shoes, she would try to kill him without hesitation.

For the next fifteen minutes, Alicia walked around her living room, thinking about how people could get to her. If her plan was going to work, she had to protect herself. Jacqueline had already tried to kill her, Jacques Bourlia had tried to kill her, and Joseph had attacked her already, thinking she had his daughter. She realised just how lax she had been regarding her protection. She had bodyguards, but they were of no use against powerful witches.

"How the hell could I be so stupid?" she asked as she paced around the room. She stepped out onto the balcony and looked down below. This always seemed to give her some kind of perspective. As she looked at the buildings, the cars, and the people below, she thought about how vulnerable a position she had put herself in by not taking as many precautions as possible when she was doing business, dealing with other witches such as Aunt Gen *I even had all the witches from Scotland in my apartment for Christ sakes* she thought to herself shaking her head.

Alicia quickly walked through her apartment up to the mezzanine, walked to the faraway bookshelf and pulled out a book she hadn't looked at in years. It was her grimoire, one her father had helped her to make and one that had been sacred to her. She pulled out another book and felt the energy of it as soon as she touched it. It brought tears to her eyes immediately. It was her father's grimoire, another book she hadn't picked up in years, not since he had died. She brushed her hand gently over her father's book and felt the embossed leather symbols he had created. It was a beautiful black leather book bound by a specialist bookbinder from Italy. Her father had flown him over and let him stay with them for two weeks until he was completely satisfied. Her father had insisted on flying the same bookbinder over from Italy when it was

Alicia's turn to create her grimoire. She had spent weeks thinking about the cover. She had settled on a heritage blue-coloured leather with a damask pattern gold leafed into it. In the centre was a pentagram adorned with a blue sapphire gemstone. It had cost over fifty thousand dollars to make the 500 blank-page book, but Alicia adored it when she was younger. She had taken care not to write anything frivolous in the book and had always practised what she would write on a separate sheet of paper before copying it into the book. This way, she could make all the mistakes she needed before the final version ended in the book.

She gently thumbed through the pages of her book before going to the back to look for spells and incantations for protection.

She felt like a fourteen-year-old girl again, enjoying being by herself and poring over the pages of her grimoire. Her phone rang several times, but she ignored it.

She realised she had decided as she sat cross-legged, barefoot, wearing old jeans and a sweater, going through her grimoire. She was looking for protection spells to be placed on herself and her energy to do what she'd been thinking about for years. People were out to get her, to harm her or even kill her. She had to be extremely careful.

She picked up the two heavy books that felt like carrying concrete slabs downstairs and went to the couch to get more comfortable. As she picked up the books, she saw her mother's grimoire, which she could never bring herself to look through as she got older. Maybe this was the day. She would have had protection spells, too.

She ignored more phone calls and reached over the breakfast bar to silence her phone; she didn't want to be interrupted.

Alicia spent the next few hours reading all she could from her father's grimoire and her own. She recognised the child-like writing in the early entries of her book and could almost feel herself growing up the more she read through her later spells in the books. There were little drawings in the margins of the pages, some comments at the bottom, and Alicia's personality was all over it.

Her father's book was a little different. It was measured, precise and devoid of any personality. It was what it was: a book for information only and to record new and exciting spells.

The books sucked her in, and time just seemed to stand still. She looked at the entry for a protection spell she had written when she was a little older:

The Shield of Seraphic Guard.

Purpose: To envelop the caster in a protective aura, shielding their energy from malevolent influences and psychic harm.

INGREDIENTS:

A circle of salt for purity and protection

Three white candles representing peace, protection, and purity

A small amulet or crystal for personal energy focus

Lavender or sage, for cleansing and peace

RITUAL:

Begin at the twilight hour, where day meets night, symbolising the balance between light and dark.

Form a circle with salt, large enough to sit within comfortably. This circle acts as your sacred space, a barrier against negativity.

Place the three white candles at equidistant points around the circle's edge and light them to call forth protection.

Hold the amulet or crystal in your dominant hand, closing your eyes to centre your spirit.

Recite the incantation thrice with clear intention:

"By the light of three, a shield around me,

Seraphic guard, ward and keep,

Let no harm or sorrow seep,

Against all ill, my energy seal,

In this circle, I do heal.

As I will it, so mote it be."

Burn the lavender or sage within the circle, letting the smoke purify your space and solidify the protective barrier.

Sit in meditation, visualising a luminous shield enveloping you, powered by the spell and your intent.

Close the ritual by blowing out the candles and thanking the unseen guardians for their protection. Carry the amulet or crystal as a talisman of this protective spell.

Note: The Shield of Seraphic Guard is to be cast with respect and not out of fear, for proper protection is found through balance and peace.

Judging by the notes, her father influenced this spell, but she recalled using it to good effect. She knew ritual magick was there to focus her mind and energy on the task. Now, all she had to do was think about what she wanted, and it would happen. However, she took this day to do the rituals involved. This would focus her again and stop her mind from focusing on people who wanted to kill her.

As day turned into night, Alicia had gone through six spells from her father's and her grimoire, and she felt light and powerful and could take on the world. The spells had infused her with energy and passion for her craft again, and she hadn't realised how much she had missed doing ritual magick. The five other spells she used.

Veil of the Guardian Ancients: A spell to invoke ancient guardians' protection, creating an invisible barrier that shields the caster from physical and ethereal harm.

Mantle of the Phoenix Shield: Designed to protect against extreme forces, this spell calls upon the regenerative power of the phoenix to envelop the caster in a fireproof aura, ensuring rebirth from any ashes of destruction.

Circle of Enduring Arcana: This potent spell establishes a magical perimeter around a chosen area, repelling negative energies and entities and making it a sanctuary of peace and safety.

Whispers of the Eldritch Ward: This incantation summons an ethereal ward that cloaks the caster or an object in a layer of protection, making it undetectable to malevolent eyes and intentions.

Blessing of the Celestial Aegis: This powerful protective blessing calls down celestial light to form an impenetrable shield around the caster, absorbing and neutralising any dark magick aimed at them.

She also used her favourite incantation as a mantra:

Eclipse of Shadows, Light of Might

In the space between shadow and light,
I summon the guardians of day and night.
With power drawn from the eclipse's sight,
Shield me in your embrace, both fierce and bright.
Let no harm breach this sacred circle round,
For in your strength, my protection is found.
As above, so below, let my energy be bound,
By this mantra of might, my safety is sound.
Eclipse of shadows, light of might,
Guard my spirit with your celestial light.
Through darkness, deep and challenges tight,
I stand unwavering, ready to fight.
This mantra I chant, with all my power and right,

To ward off the dark and welcome the light.
So mote it be, in the day and the night,
Surrounded by protection, by love, and by light.

As she drifted off into a deep sleep in her bed that night, Alicia felt exhausted and exhilarated simultaneously. She repeated the mantra and thought about the five sisters she had encountered earlier in the week. As she fell into a slumber, she was more sure now that she was doing the right thing.

CHAPTER 9

Genevieve walked through to the living room where Jacqueline was sitting, just staring out the window.

She looked at her sister and raised her eyebrows. "That was Joseph on the phone. He said he had spoken to Alicia, and she would not go after David. She had bigger fish to fry, she said."

Jacqueline sighed deeply, "Oh my god, that's an enormous weight off my chest. I worried that she was going to kill him."

Genevieve shook her head, "I wouldn't feel too relieved just yet. Joseph explained Alicia seems more determined than ever to destroy the Akashic records and replace them with something of her own."

"What! How on earth would she even do that?" Jacqueline said.

Genevieve shook her head again, "I don't have a clue," she said, breathing out almost exasperatedly.

They both stopped talking and just sat and stared, their thoughts swirling around their heads.

The whooshing sound broke the silence coming from the other end of the living room.

A portal circle opened, and Genevieve and Jacqueline had to stand up to see who was coming through it.

It was Terence.

"Terence! We haven't seen you in a while. What have you been up to?" Genevieve said. Jacqueline was still a little wary of the little creature.

"Getting up to no good is what I've been doing," He said, waddling over to Genevieve and joining them next to the couches.

He hopped up onto the couch and looked at Genevieve and Jacqueline. "As I told you, I think I have a way of stopping Alicia from destroying the Akashic records."

Genevieve and Jacqueline both looked at each other.

"Well, are you going to tell us or just keep it to yourself?" asked Jacqueline.

Terence snorted, "I see where your son gets his attitude from."

Jacqueline went to answer him, but Genevieve put her hand out, touched Jacqueline's arm and shot her a look.

"Go on, Terence," Genevieve said.

Terence rocked a little on the couch to get comfortable. "Well, we have figured out that for the Akashic records to be destroyed, the world's energy has to be low."

Jacqueline looked at him and nodded, "And?"

Terence looked up at Genevieve and sighed a little. Genevieve raised her eyebrows to acknowledge his frustration with Jacqueline.

"Well, right now, the ascension cannot occur, which usually happens every twenty-two years, which we've spoken about before. So..." Jacqueline interrupted Terence.

"What's the ascension? I don't know about this," She asked.

Genevieve stood up, "I'll make a pot of tea," she said. While waiting for the kettle to boil, she listened to what Terence told Jacqueline to reacquaint herself with 'The Ascension' details.

Terence looked at Jacqueline and shifted a little again on the couch. "Every twenty-two years, the human energy frequency is raised to another level, hence the name 'The Ascension'. Well, it was due to happen again this year, and preparations were underway on the seventh plane to celebrate this and prepare humans for this next stage in their growth." Terence stopped and looked at Jacqueline to make sure she was understanding.

Jacqueline looked at Terence and bent down slightly

to face him, "I can take in more information before I forget it. Just keep going until I ask questions."

They heard Genevieve chuckling in the background and turned to her. Genevieve shook her head, "One thing you need to know about Jacqueline is she hates being treated like a fool, so you're not quite seeing the best of her just now, coupled with the fact that she thought Alicia was going to go after her son."

Jacqueline sat up straight. "You don't need to apologise on my behalf, Gen." She looked back at Terence, who looked at her and then at Genevieve.

"I think I'm going to like her," he said, turning to Jacqueline.

She waited for him to continue, ignoring his comment.

"Ah! Okay. I'll continue, shall I?" Terence said.

Jacqueline rolled her eyes, smirked a little, and nodded.

"So, this year, the Ascension could not happen because the world's energy was too low to energise the Lake of Enlightenment. The lake helps to raise the energy frequency of all the seven planes," Terence said.

"So why is it so low this year?" Jacqueline asked, looking between Terence and Genevieve.

Terence nodded, "There are Lots of different reasons: wars, more government control, fear being spread in the media, stressful work life, less income for many people, more poverty. There's a lot more, but the point is, humans have been spiralling downwards in their energy frequency since 2020."

"When the first Covid cases came about?" Jacqueline replied.

"Yes, and more importantly, when the first lockdown was imposed in March 2020," Terence said.

Jacqueline's eyebrows knitted together in a thoughtful frown, "Why is that more important?"

"Well, imagine you are being forced to stay in your house by the government and the police. You would consciously think that the government is doing it for your own good, but subconsciously, you would know that the government controls you, which creates fear and panic and stresses people. This..." He didn't finish the sentence.

"Lowers the energy of the population worldwide," Jacqueline said, finishing his sentence.

"Exactly. This was the big event that kick-started the energy lowering. Add on top of that the media spreading fear around the world about global wars, government-controlled money, the CBDC, the politicians we have in power, global financial meltdown, the housing crisis, and so on and so on. It's been a constant bombardment on the energy of the human population for the last seven years, and it has finally come to a head and led us to this: the devolution of human energy frequency," Terence said, sitting back on the couch a little more.

Jacqueline shook her head. "That all ties in with

what Logan and I have found out, too. It all fits and sounds catastrophic when you put it like that," Jacqueline said.

"It is catastrophic, and unless you do something about it, it's only going to get worse over the next twenty-two years and possibly longer," Terence replied.

"You said 'unless you do something about it'?" Jacqueline said, narrowing her eyes a little.

"Well, I'm not supposed to do anything to intervene. I am a monk on the seventh plane, and I am impartial, and whatever happens will happen," Terence replied.

"But?" Jacqueline quipped.

"But," Terence paused, "I think I have found the solution to help raise the energy around the world. Which is why I came here."

Genevieve entered with a tray carrying a pot of tea, several cups, and a plate with some biscuits. "I think we're going to need this," she said, looking at Jacqueline. There was also a small plate with cooked chicken slices for Terence.

CHAPTER 10

J essica could see through David's eyes as a young
boy. David was around four when he realised he
would not see his mother and father again.

David played in his room at his Aunt
Genevieve's house four days after his mother and father
had dropped him off. She saw him playing with some
toy dinosaurs when he stood and looked out the
window. He was looking for his mother and father, and
she felt his pain when he had the thought that they
weren't coming back for him.

Jessica was lying back on the floor in the room with
David. They were practising an advanced form of
magick they had been learning for the last few weeks.
They practised getting inside each other's heads and
hearing their thoughts.

For the first few days, they sat opposite each other,
mentally climbed inside each other's minds, and could

feel their emotions. They would confirm back and forth what each of them was feeling. They then moved on to hearing their thoughts, which was much trickier. It helped that they had spent so much time together in the past as they tapped into each other's energy signature. It was tricky feeling at first, but Jessica found a way to scan David's energy mentally, and she felt a clicking sensation when she connected with David. She taught this to David, who felt it, too.

They could not hear the other's thoughts, which again they confirmed with each other as they practised.

Now, they were getting deeper and deeper into each other's minds, and it was scary for both of them. She thought the level of trust required to let David probe inside Jessica's mind was very scary for her, as it must be for David, too.

They lay on their backs in Jessica's room and mentally tuned into each other's energy signature. Both of them felt and confirmed the now-familiar clicking sound.

She had to let go a little more each time to get deeper into David's mind.

Jessica was deep inside this time, and she felt David's emotions as a child. She felt a lump in her throat as she experienced the same feeling of abandonment that he felt.

As she wandered through his memories, she could feel that feeling of being abandoned penetrate everything he did, from how he played the field with the girls and women in his life to how he didn't form deep friendships with his male friends. It was all rooted in not relying on anybody else. She realised David was a lot tougher than he made out on the surface. He was highly self-reliant.

As she probed more, she felt the elation he had felt when he first started to lucid dream. It was by accident at first, and then he became a little obsessed with the subject. She discovered he was a very skilled lucid dreamer; he just hadn't known what he could do with it and how to take it to the next level. He had tried astral projection before but couldn't quite get the hang of it.

Then she wandered into a room in his mind where she saw herself, but not her present-day self. It was back when she was around fourteen years old. David had actual memories of meeting Jessica stuck in his subconscious mind, and he didn't even know it. She had never told David the full story of how she had known of him for years before they met that night in the car park where she had saved him from getting his arse kicked by another witch. It was something that just hadn't cropped up again as things had moved so fast for David when he discovered he was a witch.

She watched David as a fourteen-year-old boy and how she had spoken to him in the astral realm. She had met him in the astral realm several times, but he would remember none of it at the conscious level as he wasn't trying to astral project; it was just something everyone does occasionally. She watched his bewilderment when he first saw her all those years ago. His emotions were all over the place: excitement at seeing another astral body for the first time, fear of what might happen to him, and the attraction he had for her back then were all clear for her to see while she watched his memories.

Just then, she felt herself being ripped out of his mind and back into the living world where they were in her room.

David turned on his side and looked at her, "What did you see?"

"You will not believe it. I wandered into the memory of when we first met about ten years ago," she said, watching his reaction.

"What! We met ten years ago?" he said, not quite believing they had met previously.

"Yes, I told you we'd been watching you because of your energy spikes way back when I first met you in the car park that night," Jessica replied.

David thought back to that night. "Jeez, yes, I remember you saying something like that, but we never spoke about it again."

"I know, it just never came up. Everything has been happening so fast," Jessica said.

David lay down again on his back, "So, we've known each other for years?"

"Yes, but we do not know each other. In the astral world where we met those few times, your personality hadn't yet fully taken shape," Jessica remarked, lying on her back.

"What did we say to each other?" David asked.

"Nothing, really. It was more of a seeing each other. I focused on your energy and overall feelings, but nothing was said. We felt your energy spikes, and I came looking for your energy," Jessica said.

"Wow, that's mental, don't you think? We've known each other for over ten years and are now friends in the physical world. That's nuts," David said slowly, thinking about the profundity of this situation.

They both continued to lie on their backs, head to head and bodies at a forty-five-degree angle to each other. They thought about the strangeness of life and pondered where their lives were headed.

CHAPTER 11

Alicia felt stronger now than she had in a long time and more sure of herself.

She had been practising the 'old' magick her father taught her as a little girl. It brought back memories of happier times, simpler times, where she was carefree and didn't have to make big decisions every day, decisions that could make her lose millions of dollars.

Alicia had locked herself in her apartment and turned off her phone for the last few days, enjoying the peace, but she knew she couldn't do this for much longer.

The buzzing from the phone startled her, signalling the concierge's call.

She picked up the phone, "Alicia speaking," she said curtly.

"Ma'am, we have Mr and Mrs Fraser in the lobby for you. Are they okay to come up?" Asked the concierge.

Alicia thought for a second, "Yes, send them up."

"Okay, ma'am," said the concierge and hung up.

Alicia quickly pulled the coffee table that was sitting on the rug to cover the pentagram and folded out the rest of the rug to cover it completely.

She heard the elevator ping as Deborah and Iain smiled warmly at her, genuinely happy to see her.

"Alicia, where the hell have you been? I've been calling you," Iain said as he walked over to her and hugged her.

Deborah kissed Alicia on both cheeks and held her by the shoulders, "Are you okay, Alicia?" with a worried frown.

"I'm fine, and I've had my phone turned off. I needed some space away from everything." She said.

Iain looked around and then directly at the grimoires lying at the side of the couch, "That's not like you. What have you been up to?" he asked, still looking at the grimoires.

Alicia looked in the direction Iain was looking and lifted her eyes to meet his gaze.

Deborah caught the look between them, "Okay, what's going on, you two?" she asked, looking at Alicia and then at her husband.

Iain's gaze never left Alicia. He spoke sternly, "Alicia, why do you have two grimoires sitting out? Have you started what you have been talking about for the last few months?"

Oddly, Alicia felt a strange embarrassment, as though caught doing something forbidden, a feeling that harked back to her childhood days. She shook off the feeling.

"Iain, we are friends, but it doesn't give you the right to question what I have been doing," Alicia said, holding Iain's gaze.

Deborah looked at the two of them and noticed the tension rising. "I'll have a drink if there's one going," She said in as cheery a voice as she could muster.

Iain was first to break his gaze.

Alicia let out a little sigh of relief, barely noticeable. She didn't need a confrontation between her and her two friends, but she would be damned if she was going to answer to Iain or anybody else.

Iain ran his fingers through his thinning hair and smiled; the smile didn't reach his eyes.

Alicia didn't miss the smile, and she wondered if he was up to something himself or if she was just being paranoid.

Deborah wandered over to the couch and sat down as Alicia walked over to the drinks cabinet to pour them a drink.

"The usual?" Alicia asked.

Iain and Deborah nodded as Iain sat down beside his wife.

As Alicia pivoted, drinks in hand, she saw Deborah

74 | STEVEN P AITCHISON

wrestling to lift a grimoire from the floor. In unison, Iain and Alicia exclaimed, "No!" their voices ringing urgently.

Alicia put the drinks on the coffee table, quickly snatched the heavy book from Deborah and bent down to pick the other one up. She struggled a little to carry them but mustered up her strength and walked toward the mezzanine. She heard Iain admonishing his wife for touching the grimoires as he explained what they were and why no one else but the owner should touch them.

As Alicia replaced the grimoires on the shelf, she heard a noise behind her. It was Deborah who had climbed the stairs to apologise to Alicia.

Alicia sighed and went to hug Deborah to let her know it was okay when she saw a flash of light coming from downstairs in the living area.

Deborah and Alicia turned around simultaneously and looked to where the flash came from.

They were in the far corner of the mezzanine, and neither could see anything from the balcony.

Alicia touched Deborah on the shoulder and hurried back down the mezzanine steps to the living area, where Iain was.

As she reached the bottom step, she stopped dead in her tracks.

A group of around six people huddled in the middle of the room, talking to Iain. They were all wearing black robes with a white collar.

Alicia knew the costumes were from somewhere but couldn't recall where. As she walked toward them, she remembered: They were the costumes of the Elemental High Council. Since the incident involving Anton Allard many years prior, she had encountered none of the group's members.

She hadn't been afraid of the High Council back then, and she wasn't afraid of them now. She was furious that Iain had obviously brought them here.

Iain spotted Alicia and held his hands up. "Alicia, this is not what it looks like," he said, trying to slow her quick strides toward the high council.

"GET OUT!" she roared, and her voice seemed to echo around the whole room. "Get out of my fuckin' home this instant."

The men in robes seemed defiant as they huddled closer together to form a unit as if in battle.

"Alicia," Iain pleaded.

Alicia held out her hand, closed her eyes and recited an incantation:

"By the forces of earth, air, fire, and sea,
Return these beings from whence they came,
Let this space be mine and mine alone,
As I will it, so mote it be."

A surge of energy thrust toward the group of men met with an immediate response as Alicia witnessed a barrier springing to life. Her magick clashed against the shield, sending sparks across the room, the invisible barrier momentarily radiating with an orange glow.

Alicia smiled as she wanted to know how they were protecting themselves. They were joining their forces, which would normally be a powerful barrier, almost impenetrable, but Alicia knew what to do in this situation.

She smiled and stood before the six men, closed her eyes and whispered to herself:

"Whispers of elements, ancient and deep,
Bend to my will, through barriers seep.
Unite your voices, gentle and sly,
Guide these guardians to comply.
By the silent power of the hidden moon,
Let their defences falter and swoon.
In their minds, plant doubt and question,
Lead them to lower their mighty protection."

Alicia then visualised a harrowing battlefield where the six men stood and looked around them. Hundreds of people were desperately trying to defend themselves against ferocious giant wolves tearing through the surrounding ranks, their howls merging with the screams of the afflicted. The wolves were ripping bodies apart all around them. The screams were horrific. Alicia amplified their terror within the minds of the men, conjuring even more wolves and carnage. Chaos reigned supreme. She intensified the scene with thunderous drumming, its crescendo paralleling the men's rising panic, before assaulting their senses with nauseating odours so potent it felt inescapable. The men's psychic barrier crumbled, their hands clutching their heads to escape the sensory onslaught Alicia master-fully orchestrated.

Alicia laughed as she recited the first incantation again:

"By the forces of earth, air, fire, and sea,
Return these beings from whence they came,
Let this space be mine and mine alone,
As I will it, so mote it be."

The men before her vanished, leaving Alicia alone in the centre of the room, hatred blazing in her eyes. She slowly turned her gaze towards Iain.

CHAPTER 12

I t was the day of the 'Final Eighteen'.

Jessica sat in her room, wondering if she would make it from the last twenty-four students to the final eighteen.

She tried to relax as much as possible and told herself it didn't matter if she got through. The fantastic knowledge she had gained from the magick academy was enough for her, and it had changed her in so many ways she wouldn't have thought possible before coming here. Her magick was the strongest it had ever been. Her mind was sharp. She was mentally tough and ready to take on any type of challenge now. Physically, she had never been stronger. Everything about her had changed for the better, and she loved the academy for this alone, but she still wanted to get through to the final eighteen.

It was something she was born with, a very strong competitive streak, and this was no different.

She hadn't exactly sailed through to the last twenty-four students but hadn't found it too difficult. This happened because everything she was learning here thoroughly enraptured her.

Two years of learning every aspect of magick, all the hard work, all the physical and mental training, all the trials, and the studying had resulted in Jessica and David being in the top twenty-four. She wondered now if she could make it to the last eighteen. She wondered what David would think now, probably lying on his bed reading a book and feeling chilled about the whole thing.

The gentle voice of Shallan, the interactive AI voice, spoke as Jessica brushed her teeth. "Jessica, you have five minutes, and they will be ready for you in the main hall for the final eighteen ceremony. Please wait just outside your door before going to the hall's centre."

Jessica's stomach flipped a little with excitement as she finished brushing her teeth, spitting water into the sink, and pulled her long red hair away from her face. "Thank you, Shallan," she said.

"It's my pleasure, Jessica. Before entering the main hall, do you want music, videos, or something else?" Shallan said.

"No, thank you. I'd prefer some silence to gather my thoughts," Jessica said.

"Silence it is," Shallan replied.

Jessica sat on the edge of the bed, waiting for the sound to signal the door opening into the main hall.

She closed her eyes, thought about David, and imagined him sitting on his bed now, waiting for the sound.

A gentle chiming now sounded throughout the castle grounds, and Jessica jumped up and waited for the doors to open.

The door gently slid open. Jessica walked confidently into the main hall and waited just outside her door. She saw the others coming out and noticed David opposite her, pushing his hands through his hair. He looked up, and a smile suddenly crossed his face. She smiled back at him.

All the students left their rooms and stayed by their door as instructed.

Jessica looked around and squinted her eyes a little. There weren't twenty-four people here. She had just started counting when a voice over the main tannoy interrupted her.

"We are now down to the last twenty-four. Some more astute students may have noticed fewer than twenty-four students here. The reason for that will become clear. Can you please walk toward the tables at the centre of the room and sit down?" The female voice from the tannoy instructed.

Jessica walked toward the table as instructed and didn't feel as nervous.

As she reached the table, she pulled out a chair, sat down and waited to find out what happened next.

"When I call your number, I want you to stand up." The woman on the tannoy said.

All the students looked around the room and the tables, wondering what was happening.

"Number twelve." The tannoy announced.

Two people, a young man and a woman, slid out of their chairs and stood up. All the students looked confused.

What are they up to? Jessica wondered.

"Number Thirty-nine." The tannoy announced.

Another two students stood up, a young woman and a man.

"Number thirty-three." Came the voice over the tannoy.

Jessica's stomach flipped again as she pushed out of her seat and stood up. To her amusement, she saw David standing up, smiling over at her.

The tannoy announced six more numbers, clearly showing that individuals were being paired off. Jessica pondered the criteria used for these pairings.

She didn't know the other students well enough to guess how they coupled the students. Then, a moment of dread came over her. *Will I have to battle with David to get to the next stage?*

They waited another few seconds. "Can the coupled students come together in the centre of the room and stand opposite each other."

Jessica watched as David walked toward her in the

centre of the room. He smiled, obviously not worried about what might happen here.

The nine coupled students stood facing each other in the centre of the room about three feet apart.

One instructor was there to keep them right.

Jessica fretted that she must battle against David to reach the next stage. She didn't like this and thought about not engaging in any battles with David; she would rather let him win than have to battle him. Jessica felt she had come this far and learned a ton about magick and, more importantly, about herself, so she was happy to stand aside and let David forge ahead in the trials.

The air was thick with anticipation as the instructor walked between the paired students.

She spoke with an air of authority, "What will happen next is that you and your partner will work together to stay alive, metaphorically. There will be nine quick trials now, and your job is to keep each other alive in each of the trials. Different rooms will host the trials, and the room will automatically transition to a new scene as soon as one trial concludes and eliminates someone, mirroring your experiences over the past two years. If you or your partner gets killed, you will both be out of the trials. In the last trial room, there will be four remaining students, and you will each battle to stay alive in the last setting, using your magick to eliminate your opponents. You will try to kill your opponent with magic, but do not be concerned, as your magick will only eliminate your opponent from the trials and not kill them."

The instructor walked up and down the line of coupled students and looked at them as she slowly explained what would happen. "Are you clear on what you are doing here?"

One student raised their hand.

The instructor nodded her head so the student could ask the question.

"Are we trying to kill each other or just to survive in the room?" Said the young man with curly black hair.

"Decide when you get to the different rooms."

Jessica suddenly had a thought and tried to catch David's attention. He was looking at the instructor from the other end of the line.

Jessica was anxious that she might not get his attention before they were told to go into the room.

Finally, he turned around and noticed Jessica's face, obviously looking a little distorted. He screwed up his eyes, questioning what she wanted.

The instructor was still talking as Jessica was mouthing to him.

"What?" He mouthed over to her.

"Fuck sake," she said, getting a little frustrated.

She would have to wait until they came together to tell him what she was saying.

The instructor finally stopped with all her instructions and said, "Okay, time to enter the first room."

David and Jessica walked toward each other, and David was eager to learn what Jessica was talking about.

"Kill them in front of us," Jessica whispered as soon as he was in earshot.

"What!" he said, looking in front of him and suddenly realising what Jessica was talking about.

As the door opened to the room, they could see it was a vast expanse of desert land, basically a land of nothingness and nowhere to run or hide. David turned to Jessica and nodded.

As soon as the door to the room closed, Jessica turned to David. They both raised their hands and projected a shield around them. Jessica shouted, "Shadow bind." She looked at him to make sure he understood. David looked confused for a second and then understood what she was saying.

They both started reciting aloud the spell they had each learned:

"Shadows deep and night so black,
Bind thee now, no light, no crack.
Round and round, a hex I cast,
In darkness bind, hold tight, hold fast.
Let not escape nor will to fight,
In shadow's grasp, you'll find no light.
By power's call and magic's hex,
I bind thee now, no move, no flex."

They directed the spell at the couple before them, and it worked. The young man, who had long dark hair, and the young woman, who had a shaved head, looked stunned. When Jessica and David cast their spell on them, they were bound and immovable.

The instructors had been sneaky, and Jessica felt blessed that she understood what to do at the last minute just before entering the new room. She felt blessed more that David was on the same wavelength as her and understood what she was trying to do.

They both shared a brief smile, but it faded quickly as the surrounding scene shifted with the elimination of the couple in front of them.

CHAPTER 13

"Alicia, this is honestly not what it looks like," Iain said, almost pleading. The fact that he had not told her he was an elemental witch meant that this looked to Alicia like another betrayal of trust.

The fury ran through her veins as she fought to suppress doing something to him she might regret. *At least give him a chance to explain,* she told herself.

Suddenly, she calmed within the space of a few seconds.

"Explain," she said to him.

Deborah was standing at his side, scared and confused, and looking at her husband for an explanation.

He looked at Deborah and then at Alicia and sighed, "They didn't come here for you. They were following my trail here, and it just so happens that I was in your apartment when they caught up with me."

"Iain, I don't understand; why were they looking for you?" Deborah asked.

Alicia stared at him, wondering if she should trust him for a second time.

"I've been visiting the seventh plane frequently, and the High Council wanted to know why. There was a meeting planned a few weeks ago, and when I didn't attend, they set another date for last week, and I didn't attend that one either." Iain said, looking a little worried.

"A few questions there, Iain. What were you doing on the seventh plane, and why did you not attend the meetings you had set with them?" Alicia asked, softening a little now and curious.

Iain looked at Deborah, "I was practising my magick on the seventh plane, something I haven't done for a while."

Deborah looked at her husband, a little confused and asked the question that was on Alicia's mind, "Why did you go to the seventh plane to practise magick?"

Alicia looked to Iain for answers.

"Can we sit down?" He asked.

Alicia nodded and led them to the couch area. At this moment, a beam of sunshine shone directly in front of them as if leading them.

Iain sat down and exhaled. "I've been thinking about ways to destroy the Akashic records."

He let it sink in and looked at Alicia, waiting for her to say something.

She looked at him with more scepticism now, "Why?"

"To help you!" he said.

"You're going to have to explain that one, Iain; I'm losing my patience here." Alicia shot back.

Deborah still looked worried, looking back and forth between Alicia and Iain as if something was about to kick off between them.

"I thought if I couldn't stop you from destroying the Akashic records, I could do some research and figure out how to do it with as little disruption as possible," he said.

"And, what did you find out?" Alicia asked.

Iain shuffled forward on the couch, "Well, something exciting."

"Is this why you have been away from the house as much? You've never been in for the last few weeks." Deborah asked.

He turned to her, "I didn't want to worry you, Debs."

"So what did you find out, Iain, "Alicia asked, still angry but slightly calmer than before.

"I was doing lots of magick over there, just your normal run of mill, energy magick, and had been doing it for a few weeks. Just finding out what type of reaction I got when I tried it close to the Akashic records. I discovered that the Akashic records drew energy from The Lake of Enlightenment on the seventh plane. The

Lake of Enlightenment has almost depleted because of the low energy on the Earth Plane." He looked at Alicia for a reaction.

"And?" Alicia replied.

"Well, I also discovered that the Lake of Enlightenment was one of the primary energy sources for the Akashic records. So it got me thinking: if the Lake of Enlightenment was the primary source of energy for the Akashic records and the Lake is now depleted, where is the energy coming from for the Akashic records?" He smiled and turned to Alicia again.

The wheels in her mind were turning; if *there was another energy source, I could use that to amplify my magick to destroy the Akashic records.* She looked at Iain again. She didn't know if she believed him, but she could verify this information, so she put her doubts aside for now.

"Anything else?" She asked.

"Yes, much more," he replied, now a little more animated as he had piqued her interest.

Deborah looked at her husband and looked as keen to hear about his magick adventures as much as Alicia did.

He looked at Deborah and then at Alicia and smiled again, "Have you ever heard of the Nexus of Dreams?"

Alicia frowned a little. It rang a bell for her, but she couldn't quite keep hold of the distant memory. "I vaguely recall something, but I can't think where from. What is it?"

"Well, the Lake of Enlightenment draws its energy from the Earth plane and the emotions and feelings of everyone on Earth. As you know, the energy of the people on the Earth plane is extremely low right now, making the Akashic records vulnerable. The Nexus of Dreams, which I didn't name, was from a source much higher than me..."

"What is the Nexus of Dreams Iain?" Alicia asked as she sighed. She still wasn't sure if he was making this up.

"The Nexus of Dreams is where the hopes, dreams and aspirations of every sentient being from all seven planes live. It exists within the Akashic records itself. This energy source is infinite, Alicia." he looked at Alicia and waited for her reaction.

"Why would you bring this to me and not keep the information for yourself?" Alicia asked suspiciously.

Iain sighed and stood up to face Alicia, "Okay, Alicia, I have been nothing but honest with you this whole time despite your accusatory suspicions. I know I didn't tell you I was an elemental witch, and you know the reasons, but that doesn't give you the right to be suspicious about everything I do. I am not a practising witch, but I still have the power and like to keep abreast of what's happening in the magickal world. The High Council followed me for what I was doing, not you. I have been nothing but a good friend for years, and you're seriously jeopardising our friendship with your suspicious attitude toward me. Decide. Either you trust me, or you don't?"

Alicia kept very calm as she listened to Iain and tried to decide if he was genuine. She quickly passed over Deborah's energy field as she sat on the couch, and it was clear Deborah knew nothing about what Iain was doing and his Magick activities. Alicia did the same with Iain as he got more vociferous about their friendship. She couldn't sense anything, but he could have blocked his energy from her.

Fuck this! She thought and was very close to the point of just letting their friendship go, which would mean letting Deborah go, too. She was so close, but another part of her mind opened up. *You're throwing away this friendship over what? You are being paranoid!*

Deborah stood up and joined her husband, putting her arm around his waist. This was a way to tell Alicia that she stood by her husband.

Alicia sighed and looked down before looking back at Deborah and Iain, "I'm sorry. I...I have been getting rather suspicious of everything and everyone just now. I have become obsessed with my actions and don't trust anyone now." She felt a relief wash over her as she shared these feelings with her two friends and walked over to them to hug them, which she was not prone to doing.

"You were right, Alicia, not to trust me," Iain said as he walked before Deborah. He raised his hands and closed his eyes.

An invisible force suddenly bound Alicia, and she couldn't move. She was being squeezed so tight that she couldn't catch a breath. She felt as if she was suffocating. Her mind went elsewhere and tried to cast a spell to free her from this. She was losing consciousness; she couldn't think straight. Her mind wandered in all different directions, and she couldn't focus on one strand of thought. She felt as if she was extremely drunk.

She heard distant voices in the background. It was Iain talking to Deborah.

Then everything went black. She couldn't think, couldn't see, just felt the nausea of losing consciousness. Then it all went dark.

CHAPTER 14

David and Jessica were now stuck in a forest setting. A tannoy-like voice informed the students that they had to reach the safety of the hut at the edge of the forest within the next hour to progress to the next stage.

David and Jessica exchanged bewildered glances. "Is this all they're providing?" Jessica asked, frustration edging her voice as she raised her hand to activate the black stopwatch on her wrist.

The mist rolled through the trees, creeping up on them slowly like a rabid dog weighing up its prey. They could barely make out the other pairs of students, looking around them anxiously.

Jessica recited a spell to put David and herself in a protective bubble to stop sudden attacks. When she finished, they saw a barrage of tiny lightning bolts bounce off the energy field Jessica had just created for them.

"What the f..." Jessica gasped, looking up.

David whirled around, trying to see where the lightning bolts were coming from. It was like a barrage of tiny lightning arrows trying to get through their defences. Then, they both watched as a swarm of fairies rushed from the skies toward them. David held out his hands and sent out a mind energy spell to strengthen the bubble that Jessica had created. Jessica, too, had raised their defence by trying to place an invisible spell on them but quickly realised that wouldn't work as the bubble of protection was visible to these fairies, so it didn't matter if they were invisible. She berated herself, and David held his own to strengthen their defences.

Jessica quickly looked out to look for the other pairs of students. She couldn't see anybody now, with the mist rolling around the forest floor.

Startled, Jessica leapt as an unexpected voice echoed within their protective bubble.

"This is not a very effective form of defence now, is it, if I can get through it?" the voice said.

After looking frantically around them, they spotted a tiny fairy-like creature hovering.

"Thryline!" David said, looking at the tiny Phyton and smiling.

Jessica leaned forward and looked closely at Thryline.

"I presume you're Jessica," Thryline said, smiling at

Jessica's face. "We've not got much time. I shouldn't be helping you here, but when I saw it was you, David, I felt delighted. Now follow me and keep your protective shields up. I will help you with this." At this, Thryline waved her hand and turned it around. As they walked, a shimmering light lit up the inside of their protective bubble.

"Will that not give away our position?" Jessica asked.

Thryline looked down at Jessica, "No, it lights our way but is not visible from outside your protective shield. We're good as long as you keep that protective shield strong."

Jessica nodded.

"Where are we going?' David asked as he continued looking around him like a commando in a combat zone.

Thryline looked at him with disdain, "To the hut at the edge of the forest, of course."

"Okay, calm yourself, I'm only asking," he said, smiling.

"I thought you would have learned more by now, but you're still asking silly questions." Thryline retorted with a hint of banter in her voice.

"And you're still a pain in the arse." David shot back.

Jessica felt slightly jealous at their playful interaction as she followed Thryline through the forest.

They could see the tiny bolts of lightning continuing to flood the forest as a swarm of fairies played their role in trying to whittle down the students in this trial.

They then tried another tack. Like a swarm of birds

flowing in unison, the fairies swooped around and down together toward something on the forest floor. Jessica presumed it was one pair of students.

Jessica surmised the fairies had eliminated nobody yet as they were still in the forest. *But maybe this is different.* Maybe their only goal was to get to the hut at the forest's edge. The thought that the last of the student pairs to reach the hut would mean elimination increased her anxiety and pushed her to move faster.

"Shit! Look at that." David shouted, turning to his left side.

Thryline and Jessica stopped suddenly and turned toward a massive aircraft approaching them. On the front of the craft was a symbol that looked like a crescent moon with two teardrop shapes coming from the bottom. Jessica vaguely recognised the symbol, but it was missing something.

"Quick, run to the left!" David shouted.

"No! stay there." Jessica shouted back. Jessica closed her eyes and felt slightly panicky, but she knew they had to stay where they were as she figured this out. It was on the edge of her mind. Suddenly, it popped into place, like a jigsaw piece slotting together.

"Jeezus Jess, come on, it's heading straight for us," David said, trying to run away from the aircraft. Jessica quickly strengthened the protective bubble they were in and continued.

The aircraft was approaching fast and looked more

menacing the closer it got. The noise from the engine was deafening.

Jessica was steadfast and didn't waver. She knew what she had to do but didn't know if it was right.

"Jess!" David shouted above the noise of the aircraft.

Thryline hovered, didn't move, and watched Jessica and David's interaction. She didn't seem anxious.

Jessica stood and cast an outward spell to draw a large teardrop in the centre of the crescent moon between the other two teardrops.

The aircraft was now only ten feet away from them and could plough through them any second.

As soon as the new teardrop appeared on the aircraft, it disappeared.

They both let out an enormous sigh of relief.

Once they had caught their breath, Jessica turned angrily toward David, "We have to fucking trust each other, David. I don't need you panicking and shouting in my ear, putting me off. Everything that happens here is a test, and we must consider how they will test us." She said, brushing some strands of her red hair away from her sweating face.

Jessica turned away and continued walking toward them. David followed her. She heard him apologising in the background as she focused on where they were going.

"Oh no, that's not good," Thryline exclaimed, looking down at the forest floor.

Jessica and David looked down and watched in

horror as millions of tiny ants swarmed inside their protective bubble. They were red ants.

Jessica brushed her legs frantically as they crawled all over her body. She slapped and brushed as many of them off as possible, but the more she brushed, the more they would appear.

David danced around the bubble, trying to get them off his arms and neck. "Ya bastard!" he shouted as he swatted more and more of them.

"I'm going to have to drop the shield," Jess shouted.

"Jess, No!" David screamed back, and then he stood perfectly still. "Think about what you just said. They are testing us."

Jessica looked at him with wide eyes. Then she closed them and stood still.

The pair stood still and remained calm as the ants crawled all over them.

It's in the mind. I choose what I feel. I choose what I see. She said to herself, thinking about the lecture from Aleister Crowley. He had described magick as 'The Science and Art of causing change to occur in conformity with one's will.' Jessica now willed a different feeling than ants crawling all over her. She focused on standing on the sand on a beautiful beach in the Bahamas, where she had been with her father to St. Kitts. The more she focused, the less she felt the crawling. Then she thought about her father and wondered what he was doing whilst she was over here. These thoughts led to other thoughts of her mother and her childhood. Like branches from a tree, the thoughts kept flowing.

Jessica opened her eyes and noticed David was looking at her and smiling.

She burst out laughing, "It worked!"

Thryline was hovering above them and smiling. "This is my cue to leave you both. David, it was nice seeing you again, and I'm sure we'll see each other again soon. Jessica," She said, smiling and looking directly at Jessica, "It was a pleasure to meet you. David spoke about you a lot when he was going through the trials. I can see why he is so fond of you. Stay strong for each other." At this, Thryline disappeared out of sight.

Jessica turned to David. "She is lovely." There was a brief silence between them. "I'm sorry I got angry at you back there," she said.

"Don't apologise. I should know to trust you one hundred per cent, so I'm sorry for doubting you." David replied.

They continued to walk when David looked up and pointed.

It was a hut about a hundred feet in front of them.

They both started running.

"Shit!" David said as he sped up and started sprinting. Jessica looked at where he was looking. She saw some of the other students sprinting for the hut, too. It seemed all the student pairs had seen the hut, and it was now a race to see who could get there first.

They sprinted as fast as they could. Jessica overtook David.

They were about ten feet away now, and pairs of students had already reached the forest hut, looking out to see who else would reach them.

Jessica was two feet away from the hut when she spotted another student beside her, and she threw herself inside as if she was about to score a try in rugby. She rolled onto her side so she wouldn't hurt herself but felt a stab of pain in her elbows and knees, but it didn't matter. She was in.

She looked out just in time to see the other students.

She watched David as he was about to do a spectacular rugby dive into the hut when he halted in midair.

"Shit!" Jessica exclaimed as she realised one of the other students must have used some kind of spell on David.

Another two students dived past David and got inside the hut.

Jessica looked around and counted fourteen other students. She then looked out at David, who had his arm out, throwing himself into the hut, only he was stuck in midair.

Jessica frantically racked her brain on how to fix this. *How to unblock a spell?* She asked herself.

It seemed like minutes she was trying to think, but she knew it must have only been seconds.

She reflected on her time in Mesopotamia and the

teachings she had received there. She knew how to unblock a spell cast on herself but not how to lift a spell cast on someone else.

She suddenly had a thought, rushed through the onlooking students, and launched herself at David. She wrapped herself around his body, quickly reciting something to herself. They both dropped to the ground like stones and shouted out in pain.

They then both jumped up to run for the hut again, just as another student was about to throw herself into it.

CHAPTER 15

Wrapped in utter darkness, she realised she had transcended her physical form but was still trapped in an abyss. *I'm going to kill Iain Fraser,* she vowed, her consciousness drifting between the tangible and the void.

She tried to get her bearings, but she felt lost. *How has he done this?* she asked, trying her hardest to think of a way out.

As time passed and Alicia's mind drifted, disconnected from her body, she became increasingly frantic at the thought of being stuck in the dark void.

After a while, Alicia realised she was drifting in and out of sleep, or what seemed like sleep. Thinking about it rationally, she thought she couldn't fall asleep as sleep was just a form of losing consciousness. She wouldn't need sleep if her consciousness floated around in the ether. This led her on a train of thought that led to asking herself where her consciousness was going when it felt like she was falling asleep.

She had nothing else to do and tried to stay as calm as possible but followed where her mind went when she fell asleep or what felt like sleep.

She couldn't quite hold on to the thoughts as she fell asleep but kept practising, determined to find out if it led to anything.

After a while, she couldn't tell how long, as she didn't have a sense of time in this place. Alicia followed her thoughts just to the point of falling asleep.

Just like she had practised lucid dreaming when she was younger, she remained conscious on two levels: the dream world and the real world. So it was in this space she remained conscious on two levels: the darkness and sleep world.

As she stepped into the dream world, her vision suddenly came back. She could see light again.

She squinted her eyes against the sun and was aware she was lying on her back in a field. She opened her eyes to see blue skies and felt long green grass around her. A gentle breeze washed over her body, cooling her. She sat up and looked around her. She could see hills in the background and some type of village with white-painted houses nearby.

She lay back down again, feeling the elation of not having a care in the world. *What a beautiful life,* She thought as she hummed a tune to herself and waved her arms up and down at her side, feeling the soft grass. She took a deep breath and smelled the fresh smell of clean air, grass and wood burning somewhere in the distance.

She smiled to herself.

As she lay, she heard someone calling her name.

It was faint at first, but she heard someone calling out, "Alicia, come and get something to eat."

She jumped to her feet, looked down, and saw she wore a breezy summer dress, its fabric adorned with vibrant floral patterns that danced in the gentle breeze. The dress, with its delicate spaghetti straps and flowing hem, accentuated her graceful movements as she walked toward the voice of her mother.

My mother? She thought. That thought disturbed her. *Why would I question it was my mother?* She wondered.

"Coming, Mom!" She shouted back as she gracefully walked through the field, holding out her hands to feel the delicate rushes of the grass.

She continued humming a cheerful song as she walked toward her mother. She thought her father would be home soon and that they could all eat together. Alicia felt a swelling inside her stomach and realised it was pure happiness.

As she walked toward her mother, she felt a stabbing pain on her side. She looked down to see blood on her dress. The dark stain contrasted starkly with the light cotton material. She watched in horror as the blood spread across the dress.

"Mom! Mom!" She screamed as she ran toward her mother.

"Alicia!" Her mother shouted, running toward her, "What is it? What's wrong?"

"Mom!" Was all Alicia could shout as she tried to run faster toward her mother. She found she was running faster but wasn't getting closer to her mother. *What's happening to me?* She thought as she kept on running. The surrounding scene was changing. The skies were darkening.

Still running and looking down in horror as more and more blood spilt from her body. The dark skies opened up, and rain fell heavily, instantly soaking her. The blood flowed, the rain fell, and her mother shouted louder. It was overwhelming. What's *happening?* She kept asking herself. She didn't know what to do. Thunder reverberated around in her head as streaks of lightning split the dark skies. Water dripped from her face as she tried to keep running to her mother, but somehow, she knew it was useless.

I'm dying! She suddenly realised. *This is not me. I'm not a girl. I'm dying somewhere.* She looked down at her blood-soaked dress again and touched the warm, sticky substance.

Her whole body now felt cold and was getting colder by the second.

Alica stopped walking and looked up at the skies. Rain streamed down her face. The skies were now black and angry, and the lightning was streaking closer and closer toward her.

She screamed as a flash of lightning earthed about two feet away.

This is it! She thought.

She stood still and then fell to her knees. She was weak and losing this world she was in, wherever this was. It was such a beautiful moment. A moment of being carefree, with no stress and a moment of love where her mother stayed. She clung to that feeling of love for a few milliseconds more before she collapsed on the ground in front of her. Still barely awake, she watched the blood flow around her body.

Alica Collins closed her eyes. For the last time, she thought, as her eyelids were heavy, but she heard a faint voice in the background.

"Alicia!"

She tried her hardest to open her eyes again but didn't have the strength.

"Alicia, you're going to be okay." She was just able to hear.

Dad? Dad, is that you? The voice in her mind said the words didn't reach her mouth.

Darkness again.

The sounds of words echoed in some distant chamber of her mind, but she couldn't discern the words; they were just sounds clashing together.

CHAPTER 16

They both looked out of the hut after they had thrown themselves in. They were just in time to see the last student throwing herself in, but she suddenly vanished.

Jessica and David looked at each other and laughed with relief; they had just reached the next stage.

The pairing of the student who vanished also vanished, leaving fourteen students.

They were each given some food: fruit, a piece of cold meat and a bottle of water. All the students devoured their food and water. Each pair also received a bag of provisions for the next stage.

As the last of the students finished eating, the surrounding scene changed.

The remaining fourteen students were now in what looked like the Tundra regions of Russia. David looked around him and could only see frozen land, some snow-covered.

He was suddenly aware of his breath. His breath hitting the cold looked like he was smoking one of those old vapes that people puffed on a few years ago. The hot air from his lungs met resistance with the cold air of the Tundra region and produced a flowing cloud of condensation.

He wondered if this was another mind challenge to see if they could stand the cold.

It looked like the other students were far enough away that they couldn't talk to each other. They waited for the voice advising them what to do in this land, but nobody spoke.

"I think this might be a mind game here, Jess," David said as he spun around, looking for any type of rock formation to shelter in.

"I fucking hate the cold," Jess said as she rubbed her arms.

David chuckled a little and watched another plume of breath come from his mouth. "We better find some shelter quickly before nightfall, or we'll freeze to death here."

Jessica was looking for an obvious place to look for shelter, but there didn't seem to be any.

"What about the hills over there? How long do you think it would take to get over there?" David asked, pointing to some hills in the distance.

Jessica thought about this for a few seconds. Then she looked down at what she was wearing—a T-shirt, jeans, and trainers—not ideal for walking through the Tundra, she thought. She then looked at David, who was wearing almost the same outfit. "I think that's as good a plan as any."

"Okay, let's go. Can you jog a bit?" David said as he started jogging toward the hills.

"I guess I'll be jogging then," Jessica said, laughing and falling in line with David.

A few seconds into the jog, David asked, "So, are you enjoying this challenge?"

Jessica chuckled, "I wouldn't say 'enjoying' is the right word for it, but yes, you know me, I love a challenge."

They continued to jog slowly and steadily, careful not to slip on the icy rocky outcrops on the ground. This kept them warm and, hopefully, got them to their destination quicker.

"So you spoke to Thryline about me while doing the three-room trial?" Jessica asked, teasing David.

"Yeah, I didn't know what else to talk about, so your name came up," David said, smiling at her.

"You seemed to flirt with her. I sense some chemistry between you two." Jessica said, which was more of a question.

"She's a fairy, or rather a Phyton," David quickly retorted. "I think the relationship would be slightly awkward, especially the physical side of things," David said, laughing.

"Didn't you tell us that when she hugged you goodbye at the three-room trials, she was the size of a human?" Jessica replied, still jogging alongside him.

"Yeah, I suppose. She is kind of sexy, though, and quite feisty as well. A bit like yourself," David said matter-of-factly.

"You think I'm sexy?" Jessica asked, knowing the answer already.

"Fuck yeah! And you know that. That's the trouble." David said.

"What's the problem with knowing that?" Jessica asked.

"Oh, nothing..." David stopped and looked up at the skies before he finished his sentence. "It's getting dark quickly. Come on, we better run a little faster. We're nearly there."

"We're lucky. If it's the Tundra, we must be here in the summer. Otherwise, it would be dark all the time if it was winter," Jessica said, falling back in line with David.

He noticed she seemed to find it easy to jog and run and not be as out of breath as he was.

After another ten minutes, they reached the bottom of the hills they had seen from a few miles away.

David spotted a cave immediately and pointed to it. "Do you think we could climb up there?"

Jessica assessed the height of where the cave was and looked for more caves. "There's one lower down over there," she said, pointing to the left of the cave David had found.

"Brilliant, let's head in that direction then." He said, climbing over some rocks.

After another ten minutes, they reached the mouth of the cave.

Jessica spoke aloud, a short incantation to light their way inside the cave, but nothing happened. She tried again, thinking she must have got it wrong somehow. Again, nothing happened.

David tried some of his magick, but nothing happened.

They looked at each other, "What the fuck, we can't use our magick in this place. That means we will not get a fire built either." Jessica said, a little stunned.

"Well, they wouldn't let us die here, would they? So let's think about this. First, we have to build a fire. Let's go further inside the cave to protect us from the winds." David said, trying to muster a bit of confidence for them.

They slowly peered inside the dark cave, their eyes adjusting to the darkness.

"It's sloping down and back. This cave must be huge." David said, looking all around.

As they crept deeper into the cave, it eventually flattened out. They could hardly see each other, and David held out his hand for Jessica. She took it as they walked side by side.

"This looks like a suitable spot," Jessica said, checking the floor area to ensure it was flat.

"Yep. We can still see anybody or anything entering the cave, so we should be safe enough. We'll need to get some things to start a fire, though. I saw smaller twigs from dwarf shrubs, dead grass, and moss outside. I just don't know if we can create a spark to ignite it." David said, looking a little worried.

"Okay, let's try," Jessica said, walking toward the mouth of the cave again.

They had gathered moss, small twigs, and grass from outside the cave and prepared it as best they could to start a fire. David had grabbed hold of two rocks and banged them against each other, but they didn't create a spark.

"It will need to be flint or quartz to get a spark. I am presuming there are not many of those rocks in this area," Jessica said.

"Shit. We need to keep trying. I'll go outside and see if I can see any other rocks. Can you keep trying here?" he asked Jessica.

"No problem." She replied.

Jessica banged the rocks together a few times but knew it was futile. She then placed the rocks down and tried an incantation spell to create a flame, just in case. To her surprise, a flame ignited the kindling that they had made. The fire was blazing in no time as Jessica placed bigger twigs around the edges, forming a conical shape.

She gratefully heated her hands over the fire before letting David know.

Before she got him, she heard him, "Holy shit! How did you do that?" She heard him shouting from the mouth of the cave.

She laughed, "It seems we have some magickal abilities here. We presumed we didn't have any at all."

He shook his head, ran to the fire, placed his hands over it and then made out as if he was going to sit on it. "My arse is freezing." He said, smiling.

They sat by the fire, ate some provisions they had gathered from the hut, and talked about nothing. They were tired.

As they got cosy and sat cross-legged on the floor next to the fire, they began dozing, leaning against each other. Just then, they heard an almighty roar that woke them instantly.

"What the fuck!" David exclaimed, jumping up and looking toward the noise. Jessica jumped up, too.

Another roar came from the back of the cave, and they heard the pounding on the ground.

Just then, the noise source became known: a giant polar bear.

David ran, and he pulled on Jessica to do the same.

"Wait!" She shouted.

"Aw fuck!" He knew what this was, and as much as his body signals told him to get out of there, he couldn't betray Jessica's trust again. He stopped and moved by Jessica's side again as they stood their ground. She was shaking. David put his arm around her and squeezed tight. They both stood together in fear as the giant animal got closer, roaring as it was closer.

CHAPTER 17

Genevieve looked at the others in the group as she relayed Terence's plan to raise the energy of the human population on Earth.

Jacqueline and Logan were sitting in the background, as was Jonathan, who was still not one hundred per cent, but he had insisted on getting out of bed for this meeting. He wanted to see the reaction of the others in the group when Genevieve told them of Terence's plan.

As she relayed the details of what Terence had told them, there was stunned silence in the room. Genevieve didn't know if it was because they didn't quite understand how it would work or if they didn't believe it could.

. . .

Genevieve looked around the room again as everyone sat and took in her words. "Would it be better if I got Terence to explain it himself?"

The group of men and women looked at her. Alastair said, "Yes, I think that would be helpful, as he is going to be the one to implement this plan, I presume?"

"Yes. Yes, he is." Genevieve said.

At this, the living room door opened, and Terence walked in, who had been listening outside in the hallway. He didn't want to make this meeting about him; he wanted Genevieve to explain it to the group first and then ask Terence to come in if they needed him. It was clear they would need Terence to explain it more.

The group sat and stared at the little creature. Some of them had already met with Terence, but most of them hadn't, so he let them have their stare before he talked.

In his deep voice, he looked at the faces of the group. "There is a signal in the brain of every human being that, once activated, can trigger a higher state of consciousness. Now, do you want me to give you all the details or the short version?" he asked the group.

Lillian piped up immediately, "The full works, please." She said whilst the others in the group nodded.

"Agreed," said Sanjeev, "I would rather know exactly how it worked, even if we might not understand it fully."

Terence shuffled, "Okay, the full details it is."

"With all the questions, this might take a while, so I'll make some tea," Genevieve said.

Terence laughed, "I've never met a group who consumed as much tea as you do."

Genevieve looked at others in the group in mock shock as they laughed at Terence's comment.

. . .

Jonathan helped her make tea and put out biscuits while Terence continued explaining his plan. They both listened to Terence's plans to better understand.

"Okay. Many parts of the brain stimulate states of higher consciousness, and as witches, you, more than most humans, know about this. Even if you don't know the names of the parts of the brain that make you a witch and how you get your higher powers, it's there and always has been." Terence said, walking back and forth in front of the audience.

Genevieve noticed Jacqueline, smiled over at her, and put her hand on her heart area. Genevieve reciprocated. She felt this would be a tremendous step in the right direction for the Witches of Scotland, not just the Dream Dancers but all Witches in every city in Scotland, Wales, Ireland and England. In her home, what was happening right here was the making of a historic moment. She felt it and knew it in her heart. She wanted to savour it and looked at Terence, who was still talking.

Terence continued walking and talking as if he were a professor at a university, "For centuries, human evolution has evolved at a steady rate, in fact, every twenty-two earth years. If you look at history books, you notice that major breakthroughs in technology, industry, business, thinking, and medicine have occurred roughly every twenty-two years. We've all benefited from these leaps in human consciousness. The exceptions to this have been major human conflicts or disasters when humans did not evolve at the deep consciousness level." Terence looked out at the group to make sure they were getting it.

Terence's words enraptured the group. Genevieve and Jonathan laid trays of tea and biscuits on the coffee table for the group to help themselves, which some did.

Terence continued once everyone had settled back down on the sofas and chairs.

"So when humans have not evolved, there is usually not enough vibrational energy from the minds of humans to feed the Lake of Enlightenment on the seventh plane..." Terence was interrupted and stopped talking.

"What is the Lake of Enlightenment?" Asked Caroline.

· · ·

Terence nodded, "Of course, I forgot this is all second nature to me, so please stop me when you have questions. The Lake of Enlightenment sits on the seventh plane and is there to disperse the energy required to help humans evolve every twenty-two years. So, the vibrational frequency of the human mind is elevated to another level, usually every twenty-two years. However, the Lake of Enlightenment gets its energy from the human minds on earth. It uses its vibrational energy; if it is too low, the Lake of Enlightenment dissipates and cannot ascend to higher vibrational energy. Humans will not progress to the next stage of their evolution." He stopped to let this sink in as he could see the group struggling with these ideas.

To the group's surprise, the usually quiet Myra spoke up, "So, how long has the Lake of Enlightenment been around?"

"Forever!" Terence replied, "You've got to understand that the universe you exist in is only one. You have seven planes in your universe, and your universe contributes to the collective consciousness, which is the consciousness of all the existing universes."

"So, how many universes are there?" Alastair asked.

. . .

"There's an infinite number of universes," Terence replied, which was met with frowned foreheads all around.

Genevieve interjected, "I think we're getting off track here. I've told you before that Terence is a monk on the seventh plane with vast knowledge of our universe and others. As interesting as that is, we must stay focused on what we on earth have to do to stop us from falling into chaos."

Terence looked at the group for agreement before he started his explanation again.

"So this earth year, the Lake of Enlightenment completely drained of energy, for the first time since the major energy crisis of 1910 to 1954. This means humans must wait another twenty-two years before the next ascension. However, there have been no major world wars or events except for the pandemic that possibly created in the 2020s. We soon realised that the media, such as newspapers, television, radio, the internet, etc, was responsible for the devolution of the human mind, and it is getting worse."

. . .

"Wait, hold on, that's a big statement you made right there. You're saying someone created the pandemic, and the media are controlling our energy?" Marie asked in disbelief.

Terence frowned a little, "I thought you all knew this?" he said, looking at Genevieve.

Jonathan said, "We had an idea of what was happening, but you have just confirmed what we all feared."

The group nodded in agreement and looked to Terence for more.

Terence shook his head, "Oh, it gets worse, but as Gen said," He looked apologetically at Genevieve for calling her Gen with a smirk on his face. "We're here to talk about this crisis. So, if the lake of enlightenment cannot evolve the human minds on earth, it means stagnation. It means if we can lower the human energy even more, we are essentially devolving as humans, and if the energy is so low, some groups could take control by destroying the Akashic records, which is essentially the end of humans as we know it." He stopped again to let this information seep into their consciousness.

The group looked like they had a hundred questions as they processed this information.

"So, what's your way to stop this from happening?" Asked Sanjeev

"I'm glad you asked. As I mentioned, you can temporarily elevate your brain to another level of consciousness. We see this in advanced meditators and, of course, by using various man-made and natural substances here on earth. But frequency can also stimulate a part of the Vagus nerves in the brain that will lift our consciousness to another level, not just for a few minutes or hours, but for days." Terence said, waiting for questions.

"Okay, the obvious question is, what is the Vagus nerve?" Asked Marie.

"The vagus nerve is the longest and most complex of the 12 cranial nerves in the human body. It originates in the brainstem and branches to multiple organs, including the heart, lungs, and digestive tract. Importantly, it interfaces with pathways from the gut to the brain.

Studies show vagus nerve stimulation can synchronise neural oscillations in the thalamus and prefrontal cortex. This enhances thalamocortical rhythms associated with increased consciousness, attention, and arousal.

Some theorise Vagus nerve stimulation helps induce transient hypofrontality - decreased prefrontal cortex activity - similar to that seen in advanced meditators. This lets conscious experience become more unconstrained, expansive and intuitive.

By interacting with heart rate, the vagus nerve may stimulate the release of DMT, a powerful psychedelic compound that exists naturally in the human brain by the pineal gland - the neurotransmitter linked to vivid, mystical states and a subjective 'higher' consciousness.

Through such mechanisms and modulating key neurotransmitters like acetylcholine and serotonin, targeted vagus nerve stimulation could theoretically trigger elevated states of consciousness and self-awareness resonating with a 'higher' function."

"My god, that was a big brain dump right there. I didn't understand a word of that." Alastair said laughing.

"It's okay not to understand it as long as you know it exists. Stimulating the vagus nerve will talk to the whole body, including your heart, gut, and brain. And that's the key part. Most humans don't know that your heart and your gut are brain centres in your body, and it's not just the brain that controls you and your body. Again, that's for another time." Terence said to stop for a breath.

"So how do we stimulate this Vagus nerve?" Lillian asked.

"The same thing that's bringing down our energy levels - the media."

"What!" A few of the group exclaimed at once.

.   .   .

"I know, very sneaky. However, we use the signal stations to transmit the media and send another frequency out simultaneously to stimulate the vagus nerve."

"You totally lost me," Marie said.

Terence stopped walking back and forth and stopped in the middle of the room, "We are going to use television, mobile phones, radios, and computer screens to emit a certain frequency to stimulate the Vagus nerve. When we do this, we lift the consciousness of everyone in contact with that signal to lift the world's energy, which will stop the Akashic records from being destroyed." He said, a little pleased with himself but looking at the confused looks of everyone in the group.

Genevieve smiled at the group's reaction. She knew they would need time to let the information sink in, and in the meantime, there would be lots of questions for Terence.

CHAPTER 18

"Alicia. Alicia, can you hear me?" The voice said.

Alicia was still in darkness. *Are my eyes open? Where am I?* Were the questions swirling around her head just now. *Whose voice is that?* She heard it again, somewhere off in the distance. It was calling her name.

"Alicia, it's Joseph. Can you hear me?"

Joseph? Who is Joseph? Where am I? There was an endless blackness. She felt more awake now, but she still couldn't quite grasp what was happening and why she was there.

Then, suddenly, there was a dim light in the distance. She could see it or sense it; it was lighter.

Alicia's awareness of her body sharpened. Meanwhile, the voice, tinged with a Scottish accent, continued to address her, increasingly grating on her nerves.

She felt like she was lying down somewhere soft. *Am I back in the field? Where's my mother?* She searched her memory banks for any clues about what was happening here.

Iain Fraser came into her mind, then Deborah's shocked face. *Iain. Iain.* She tried to hold onto the thought, which came to her like a flash of lightning. *He attacked me and put me into a bind of some kind. That fuckin' snake.* Just as the emotions of anger tore through her, a flood of light hit her eyes as she tried to pry her eyes open.

She quickly closed them again and raised her arm over them.

"Alicia, are you okay? Are you back with us?" Joseph asked, gently placing his hand on her shoulder.

She could feel his touch.

She tried again to open her eyes. Slowly, she opened one eye. She could make out the blurred image before her, but she couldn't tell it was Joseph. Only in his voice did she recognise it was him.

There was another few minutes of drifting in and out of consciousness.

She felt more aware of herself now, and her closed eyelids were getting used to the light. She opened her eyes again and saw Joseph's shape more clearly.

"Jos..." She coughed and spluttered. Joseph gently touched her back and lifted her to sit. He put a glass of water to her mouth, which she gratefully took.

"What happened?" She asked, now sitting up.

Joseph ran his fingers through his greying hair. "I have been trying to contact you and sensed something seriously wrong. So I ported over and found you on the floor. I thought you were dead. Do you know what happened?"

"Iain fuckin' Fraser is what happened." She said with venom and held her hands to her head as it suddenly felt as if it was about to blow.

"Here, drink this water," Joseph said, holding a glass of water for her.

After another fifteen minutes, Joseph sat in the living area as she wandered through her bedroom. She wore a Burberry Cashmere housecoat and snuggled into it as she walked over to the couch. She sat down and tucked her legs up under her thighs.

Joseph replayed how he had found her. She was grateful to him as she might have died had he not, but she was already plotting how she could get to Iain and just kill him. There was no question in her mind that he would die soon. She wanted Joseph out of her apartment so she could shower and plan what to do next. She still felt groggy and fell asleep again as Joseph sat opposite her.

When she awoke again, she was lying in bed and slightly disoriented. Her head was much clearer, and she felt more rested, more herself again. She groggily looked over at her clock and moaned. She saw a note from next to the clock and picked it up:

Alicia,

I checked you over, and you seemed okay—just exhausted. I put you into bed. Hopefully, you're feeling better. I'll call you later. I'll also do some digging into Iain's whereabouts.

Joseph x.

She smiled as she swung her legs over the bed and slouched over. After shaking the last of her grogginess, she took a long, cold shower.

Whilst drying herself off, she realised she didn't even know what day it was. *How long have I been out for?* She wondered.

Walking into the living area, she quickly turned on the TV, immediately switching to CNBC. When she saw the date, she gasped. "Two days, I've been out for two days."

She spent the rest of the day returning to feeling normal, or as normal as she could feel. She took some cognitive enhancers to keep her alert. Specially crafted for her, these 'cogs' catered to her body's hormone levels and her desired emotional state. They sprang into action within thirty minutes, reigniting that familiar spark within her.

She sat on the sofa, took a deep breath and prepared herself for what she might see. She closed her eyes and whispered an incantation that would help her see exactly what happened:

Forces of time, turn back in kind
Unveil the truths left behind
I summon memories once seen

Play them back as if on-screen
After darkness overtook my sight
Reveal events in island's light
Past the haze and void of black
What happened hence show now back
By the power of time's own laws
Heed this witch's summoning call
As I will it, so must it be
Replay those lost memories to me!

In front of her, she saw the events that had happened in her living room, which she remembered. What she couldn't have known was what happened after she had blacked out.

She watched the scene before her as Deborah had her hand over her mouth, and she had nothing to do with this. She was muttering something to Iain, who admonished her angrily.

She then watched as Iain walked over to her. She smiled as he bent down to shake her. "The mighty Alicia Collins," he said laughing. He turned to Deborah, "Come on, we have to get out of here." Deborah was now crying and almost hysterical. "You can't leave her. What the hell are you doing?"

The scene faded, and Alicia gritted her teeth and thought about ways to get to Iain.

Where would he be going? She wondered. She sat thinking about her next move, if she were in his shoes.

"The Seventh plane," She said aloud and jumped up, preparing herself mentally to go to the seventh plane. Was he trying to destroy the Akashic records? What was his plan? She wondered as she rushed to the bedroom to put on some clothes. As she put on her clothes, she thought about the conversation they had had before he had attacked her, 'The Nexus of Dreams, ' she recalled him saying. *He had said it was another source of energy. Was he drawing his energy from there?*

CHAPTER 19

The giant polar bear stood on its hind legs and roared again, saliva dripping from its fang-like teeth. It then dropped on all fours, shaking the ground as it did so.

"Oh, shit!" Jessica said, hoping she hadn't made a mistake. *They wouldn't let us die.* She repeated in her mind, thinking that the academy would never do something like that. However, there was that niggling doubt in her mind. She could feel David next to her. His knees trembled slightly, but he tried to hide his fear. His breathing was rapid.

He stepped in front of Jessica, which she loved but hated simultaneously. She stood forward in line with him as they faced this danger together.

The polar bear was three feet away from them, opened its mouth to roar again, and vanished.

David and Jessica looked at each other, shocked,

sighing as if they had been holding their breath for a long time.

"Jeezus Christ, man, that was too close, way too close," David said, crouching down to catch his breath.

Jessica breathed out, brushed her fingers through her hair and lightly scratched her scalp with her fingernails to calm her down.

They expected the surrounding scene to change as this task was over.

They looked around the mouth of the cave, and just then, they saw a glow coming from the very back of the cave.

"How big is this cave?" David asked, looking at the glow.

Jessica started walking toward it, "I don't know, but I am presuming we have to follow the glow for the next stage."

David followed her and walked into the belly of the cave.

The glow was getting brighter and glowed a sparkling array of purple hues.

"That is beautiful, whatever it is," said Jessica, turning to look at David.

He looked mesmerised. "It's like a laser light show," He said in a low voice, almost whispering.

The purple light bounced off all the walls and lit up the darkness like shimmering purple water.

As they got deeper and deeper into the cave, they heard the water flow.

They moved slower as they got close to the source of the water flow sounds.

Jessica stopped in front of David, "Look! It's a giant hole in the ground with water flowing into it."

David sidled up to Jessica and then moved closer to the giant hole. It was like a massive pothole, big enough for a double-decker bus to fall into. The purple glowing vapour flowed into the hole, creating a purple lake at the bottom.

Jessica peered over the edge of the hole into the lake structure. "Wow! That must be a hundred feet down." She exclaimed.

David wandered around the other side of the hole to find the source of the purple glowing vapour. When he reached the other side of the giant hole, he gently reached out his hand to touch the vapour. "Jess!" he shouted over to her. "This is not water; it's like mist, only much lighter."

"Be careful, David," Jessica said as she walked toward him.

David picked up a rock from the ground and put it in the mist. The rock floated on top of the misty vapour.

"Holy shit! Look at this." He exclaimed excitedly.

Jessica was now looking at the floating rock as it slid over the side of the hole and down into the purple-glowing lake.

David asked Jessica, "Do you think we're meant to go down?"

Jessica widened her eyes and gently shook her head, "I don't know." She looked over the edge again.

"I think this is another test of some kind. I say we just jump in." David reached out his hand as if he was steadying himself to sit on top of the mist. His hand slipped through the purple mist. "That will not work." he looked at Jessica again, "Okay, I'm going in."

"David, what the fuck!" Jessica said as David launched onto the purple mist as if going down a giant water slide.

She glanced over the side to see him hurtling toward the lake below. She could hear him screaming excitedly, and then abruptly, he stopped and there was no sound.

She walked around the hole's perimeter to see if she could see him from another angle. Nothing; she couldn't see or hear him. "David!" she shouted. She tried this several times.

"Oh, fuck!" She thought as she prepared herself mentally to jump in after him.

The purple mist cleared just then, and darkness crept in like a prowling shadow. "David!" Jessica shouted again. Again, there was nothing.

She looked over the hole's edge again, where the purple mist was flowing too, draining the light from the cave. As the mist dropped more and more to the bottom of the hole, the light drained from the top. Then she saw someone standing at the bottom, it looked like David, but she couldn't be sure. The light was flowing into him. "What the fuck," She said as she watched the figure suck up all the light from the cave into himself.

A few seconds later, as Jessica watched the last lights wink out, she saw the figure approaching her.

Then, complete darkness.

Jessica waited a few seconds before moving. *What now?* She asked herself, thinking of a strategy to get out of this and find David.

She tried again to use her magick to light up the darkness, but it didn't work. So, what are they testing us for? she asked herself. She wracked her brain for the answer. Overcoming fear? Working together and on our own? Bravery? Using our initiative? All the above? These were all the questions floating through her mind as she tried to think of how to escape this.

Jessica quickly whipped her head around toward the direction of a whisper she heard. Her heart raced as the whisper came again from the other side. She looked all around her, but she was in complete darkness. The whispering was getting louder. Jessica felt a cold sweat on her forehead.

"Jessica," The voice whispered louder now.

"David? David, is that you?" She shouted into the darkness, her heart rate quickening.

"Jessica, I'm down at the bottom of the hole." The whispering had changed to a voice, David's voice.

"How do I get to you? I can't see anything at all." Jessica replied to the voice in the darkness.

"Wait a second," David said in an ethereal voice, as if communicating in her mind.

Just then, a light emanating from the bottom of the hole illuminated the darkness in the cave.

Jessica ventured to look over the side again, and she watched the figure at the bottom ride the purple wave of light to the top of the giant hole.

She looked in disbelief as David, now standing at the edge of the hole, looked at her and smiled in his usual boyish way, only he looked slightly different. She couldn't quite put her finger on why he looked different.

"That was intense," Was all he could say as he walked toward her.

"What the hell just happened?" Jessica said, looking at him, still trying to figure out what was different about him.

"I don't have the foggiest, but I bonded with the sixth crystal." He said.

"The what? Oh, it's alright. I know what you mean." She said as she remembered David telling her about the crystals he had bonded with. She had almost forgotten about them. "So, what does it mean for you? Does it give you something, more power? or anything?"

"I don't know, but I feel different," David replied, looking a bit perplexed as if he was trying to go inside his head to figure out what was different about him.

Jessica looked at him for a few seconds. "Okay, let's get back to the cave front..."

She didn't get to finish her sentence as the

surrounding scene changed again, and now they were in a bubble with another six students.

All the students were looking around them out of the clear bubble that seemed to float in space.

"Does this mean there's only eight of us left?" Asked one student. The other students, including Jessica and David, shrugged.

The bubble-like structure was enough for the eight students to walk around without feeling too cramped or too close to each other.

Jessica looked at Anya, another student she had gotten to know during their time at the academy. "What happened in your last trial area?" Jessica asked.

Anya looked at Jessica and smiled, "We went into the sea of the Tundra, which was freezing. I honestly thought I was going to die out there. We then had to outwit some kind of shark creature."

Jessica frowned and whispered, "So we're all doing different trials?"

"What?" Anya asked.

"Oh, nothing. I'm just wondering why we're all doing different trials. David and I were in a cave with a giant polar bear." Jessica said, trying to figure out why they all did different trials.

"Are you afraid of the water?" She asked Anya.

Anya tilted her head to the side as if thinking, "No, not really, but I know Jackov is afraid of swimming, but he managed just fine in the end." Anya took a few seconds and said, "But I am afraid of large open water spaces like the sea and lakes."

Jessica nodded, "So they're testing all our fears."

Then, Anya and the other students seemed transfixed on what was happening outside their bubble.

Jessica now focused on what was happening outside their bubble. Galaxies looked like they were on fire. The heat inside the bubble was now beginning to rise as beads of sweat ran down the foreheads of the eight students.

CHAPTER 20

Terence had spent a few hours answering all the questions from the group about how to elevate the human consciousness of the world. He had also answered different questions about the universe, which was off-topic, but he was happy to do it.

Genevieve felt all the witches in the group had grown a lot since Terence had spoken to them about the threat to humanity. They had more determination than ever to help Terence with his plan.

Genevieve, Jonathan, Jacqueline and Logan sat around the dining room table in quiet contemplation of what was about to happen.

"We are going to help to save the world. Have we let that sink in?" Logan said, looking at Jacqueline.

"I know. It's pretty crazy, right? What if we don't? We could be responsible for the demise of the human population," Jonathan said, looking wistfully out the window.

"Ach, you're all melodramatic," Genevieve said, sipping her tea.

Jacqueline laughed and looked at her sister, "Gen, we're about to help Terence tap into the network of the world, literally."

Genevieve smiled, "I know. I'm just trying to play down the enormity of what's before us."

Jacqueline smiled at her sister as she took her hand, "I only hope we get David and Jessica back before it all kicks off."

"Something tells me, Jac, that David and Jessica are at the centre of it all," Logan said.

Jonathan looked at Genevieve for an answer, "I'll tell you later, Jonathan. We have to focus on Terence's plans just now."

"When do you think he'll be back?" Jonathan asked, taking a quick look at the dining-room clock, which read 11.11 pm.

"I don't know. I just hope it will be soon. I feel we'll need to do this sooner rather than later," Genevieve replied, looking at the clock.

A sudden shift in the air seemed to shake the entire house. The air suddenly became heavier, and a strange, oppressive force seemed to be all around them.

"What the hell was that, "Logan asked, looking around the room.

The others sat in their chairs, stunned by what had happened, looking at each other, mouths agape.

Genevieve stood up and looked out the window for any signs of anything. She didn't quite know what she was looking for, but anything that could give her a clue might be helpful. She watched as people in the street looked around them, so it wasn't just them who had felt it.

Logan was now putting on his jacket, "I think we should go out and find out what that was. It doesn't feel natural." he said, looking at Jacqueline.

Jacqueline looked at him. "I'll come with you then. Gen, do you want to stay here with Jonathan and phone us if you find anything?" she said, looking at her sister.

"Yes. I'll call you..." Genevieve said when her phone rang, as did Jonathan's. "It's Lillian." She clicked on the green answer button. She motioned to Jacqueline and Logan to go just now and spoke with Lillian.

Genevieve heard Jonathan talking to Sanjeev on his phone, discussing what had happened. Nobody seemed to know what it was just yet.

The oppressiveness hung in the air like a thick, invisible fog. It seemed to make everyone a little slower as if they suddenly were five times heavier than usual.

Jonathan looked at Genevieve. "What's going on, do you think, Gen? This is all very weird, more so than anything else that's happened."

Genevieve looked out the window and watched her

sister and Logan walk up to the top of Dowanside Road towards Byers Road.

Jonathan walked over to Genevieve and put his arms around her waist from behind. She rested her hand on his arms and snuggled in a little, sensing this would require them to be stronger than ever.

CHAPTER 21

Alicia had ported to the seventh plane, which she had visited several times before. This time, it was a little different. It was usually a serene space, but the air here felt oppressive. The scenery always changed; she never knew what the scene would be like on the seventh plane, but it was always a calm place.

Alicia looked around and saw that she was on what looked like the green grass mountains of Scotland that she had seen so many times on the internet. The air was warm, and there was a slight cool breeze.

As she walked and looked around her, the scenery took her breath away. She forgot for a few milliseconds why she was here as she basked in the beauty of the Scottish hills.

Then she saw the dark clouds gathering in the

distance and watched as forks of lightning split the skies.

The warm breeze suddenly turned cold as the dark clouds rolled quickly toward her.

Instinctively, she knew that Iain Fraser was behind this, and he had already started trying to destroy the Akashic records. *How do I find him?* she wondered as she continued walking. She walked toward the dark clouds, sensing this was where he was.

The air felt heavy as she walked. Another crack of thunder reverberated in the skies, and then the rain fell, just a drizzle. Alicia knew she had to find shelter. She mentally scanned the area for anything that could shelter her from the wind and rain, and she found an old bothy that felt devoid of any energetic signatures, meaning no one was there. It was just over the hill from where she was, so it wasn't too far to go.

The rain started driving down heavier just as she reached the old cottage. Alicia pushed the old grey-painted door open and almost fell inside. She shook herself off and looked around the room she was in. There was no fire or stove, just a few tables and chairs. She was grateful for the shelter and didn't mind having basic amenities. She looked around and saw pictures of the cottage in times gone by. A plaque now told climbers and walkers that this was a bothy they could use as long as they kept it clean.

The thunder rumbled directly overhead, its roar vibrating through the old bothy as if threatening to shake it to its foundations. Lightning sliced through the dark sky, illuminating the room in brief, stark flashes as it struck alarmingly close. Peering out the small window, she squinted into the storm's chaos and saw a silhouette advancing toward the cottage through the night.

"What the hell is going on here?" She said out loud to herself.

She hurried to the cottage door and opened it to get a better view of the person. *Is this Iain?* She wondered.

She watched as the figure got closer. The rain was now lashing down on the cottage roof, creating a calming, soothing sound, and Alicia seemed mesmerised, almost hypnotised, as she watched the figure get bigger the closer they got.

She could now decipher that it was a male, by his gait and his clothes. She still couldn't make out if it was Iain or not.

Going deeper into a trance-like state, all she could do was stare at the figure walking in front of her. Her mind felt paralysed somehow. It was like being lost in a long stare that was extremely difficult to break. She now realised that, unlike a satisfying stare, she could not break this. She was indeed being hypnotised somehow.

Her mind was now drifting, too, and she couldn't focus. She plumped herself down on the step of the cottage's front door and watched the man walk toward her, cutting through the vertical rain.

Her arrested mind suddenly jolted awake as the

man walking toward the cottage was now in front of her.

"Anton Allard?" Was all Alicia could say.

The man smiled at her, a warm smile that shone through his eyes. Alicia's eyes immediately started tearing up with anger.

"Alicia, what you are about to do will see you dying." her father said.

Alicia couldn't speak and stared at the man or image before her.

After a few seconds, Alicia said, "I know this isn't real, so why are you here?" She asked him, trying to remain as calm as possible.

"I told you. This is a warning. What you are about to do will see you dying." He came closer to her, but Alicia instinctively stepped back. She didn't trust this man, even if it was an illusion. She was on the seventh plane, where magick was all around her, unlike on the Earth plane.

Anton wandered over to one of the small wooden tables, dragged out a chair and sat down, looking up at her.

Alicia followed suit and joined him at the table and opted to entertain the idea that this was Anton Allard speaking to her, the man she had castrated all those years ago, the man who had abused her as a child, the man who turned Alicia against the world.

She was growing angrier by the second and tried hard to stop herself from killing him there and then,

THE WITCHES OF SCOTLAND | 149

but he'd come with some kind of message. "Okay, what am I planning to do?" Alicia asked him, gazing at him in case he suddenly moved.

The man laughed condescendingly, the way she hated as a child but had forgotten everything until now.

"You're planning to destroy the Akashic records and install a new version, which will not work. When you do this, the whole of humanity will be destroyed. Not immediately, of course, but over time, you will be responsible for the destruction of human life as you know it. You will not have the power you once had, your money will be worthless, and savages will overtake your home. You will, of course, still have your magick powers, but all you will do is use that to defend yourself, and in time, those powers will dissipate, too." He said, smiling at Alicia as if he'd stalemated her in a chess game.

"What will happen if I don't destroy the Akashic records and install my new version, which I can do?" Alicia asked, wondering why she was even speaking to this vile man in front of her.

"You can carry on living this amazing life and be the queen of the human world, with power, money, glory and all you could ever want except love," he said, looking directly into her eyes.

Alicia squinted. "Why not love?" she asked, a bit perplexed, thinking this was a strange thing to say.

"I think I ruined that," he quickly replied.

Alicia's veins ran cold. It was all flooding back to her

now; she had tried to repress it, especially just now, but it was coming in waves. The hatred grew inside of her. Memories flitted in and out of her mind. The parties they used to have at their home, her mother, all the relatives, and the abuse at the hands of this man.

Alicia felt dread wash over her. What the hell was going on, she demanded, but no answers came to her. She felt that this man was about to answer those questions for her.

"It was me, Alicia," Anton said, looking down at the table. "I am the one who destroyed your mind all those years ago. I took something good and turned you into a little ball of hatred for men and human life, and I can't undo that, but I can try to convince you to stop what you're about to do."

The rain hammered down on the cottage's roof, thunder hammered the skies outside, and lightning splintered the darkness.

She didn't want to pour over all the memories again and forced herself to stop thinking about them. The rage was bubbling inside her, ready to explode at any second.

"I loved your mother, Alicia, but I couldn't be with her. She had devoted herself to your father, the wonderful humanitarian, the man who'd left his fortune to you, even though we had agreed that I would get twenty per cent of his stakeholding," Anton said, not taking his eyes off Alicia.

Alicia could feel herself going red with fury. She

needed to hold out longer to discover something she had always wanted to know.

Anton looked at her and smiled. "I know what you're thinking," he said, leaning on the table. "Or rather, I know the question you have."

Alicia turned to look at him again and slowly said, "How did my father die?"

Anton laughed, "That's the question right there. It cuts right to the bone, no messing." He stopped laughing and locked eyes with her. "It was me. It was me who drowned your father in that precious fucking lake he was so fond of, the one he used to take you to all the time." He looked at her, challenging her.

The words seeped slowly into Alicia's mind before the rage rose from her feet, through her legs, her body and every chakra and their powers rose through her. She screamed in a rage so loud it reverberated off the cottage's walls. With outstretched arms, she focused all her rage and power on one man, Anton Allard.

In an instant, she obliterated the man in front of her into a billion tiny pieces. She saw his face just before he exploded, that smug fucking look he used to have now tiny fragments thrown into the universe.

Then she saw Iain Fraser standing before her. He was laughing at her.

She had used all her power and directed it at Anton Allard, leaving herself momentarily vulnerable. Iain now had her bound in his own spell, and she was immobile once again at the hands of Iain Fraser.

With a flick of his hand, Iain opened a portal and transported them to the lake of enlightenment.

Alicia was bound in another spell that Iain had created, but she was still in a rage at Anton, which was now directed at Iain Fraser.

They were now both standing on the banks of the Lake of Enlightenment when Iain looked up at the skies of the vast universe above. He reached out his hand and pointed it toward the Lake, then reached out his other hand and raised it to the universes above, but he moved it as if pinpointing exactly where he wanted it to be.

Iain closed his eyes, and light started streaming from somewhere up above and through him like electricity. The grip he had on Alicia stopped, and Alicia was free again. She wondered why he had brought her up with him, knowing he would lose his power over her.

Alicia could only watch as Iain gained power from something above.

Alicia then clicked. He had spoken about the powers from the Nexus of Dreams. He was a conduit between the two powers: the Lake of Enlightenment and the Nexus of Dreams. She wanted to see how this would play out before making any kind of move on Iain.

She watched as his body seemed to swell with power. His eyes closed and looked like he was lifting a two-hundred-pound weight and straining against it. He was shaking with the strain of the power. Alicia stepped back a little. He looked as if he was about to explode.

She then turned toward the lake, which was draining.

"Oh, fuck!" Was all she could say. She didn't quite know what this meant, but she knew it wasn't good for the Earth plane, as the Lake of Enlightenment was what kept everything together, and it could also destroy the Akashic records, "What are you doing, Iain," she shouted at him.

He couldn't hear her at all. He was still under the strain of the enormous power flowing through him.

Alicia didn't know what to do. This was completely new to her.

Then, suddenly, it stopped. The lightning from above stopped flowing through Iain.

Iain turned to her and then looked back up at the universe's skies.

Alicia looked at the serene expanse of the Lake of Enlightenment, and somewhere deep inside, the Lake's energy touched her. She stood on the fragile cusp of eternity. Her gaze lifted towards the heavens that stretch infinitely above. The skies, a cosmic tapestry woven with the vibrant threads of countless universes, pulsated with the lifeblood of existence itself. Each star is a beacon of stories untold. Nebulae swirl in hues of impossible colours, shades that the human eye has never seen and the mind can scarcely imagine, painting the void with the light of creation and destruction.

The fabric of space and time seemed to fold upon itself, creating windows into other realities. Through these celestial portals, Alicia glimpsed worlds where the laws of physics are mere suggestions and realms where light is bent in reverence to the will of its inhabitants. The beauty was overwhelming, a symphony of light and shadow that sang of the boundless potential of existence.

A palpable tension marred the breathtaking vista as Iain stood at the precipice of an unfathomable decision. The air thrummed with the power at his fingertips, the potential to unravel the threads that held these myriad universes together. Dark skies flickered ominously as if aware of the impending doom, casting a haunting glow upon the lake's placid shallow waters.

At that moment, the universe held its breath, and Alicia, a solitary witness to the potential end of all things, felt a profound connection to the cosmos. In a moment of clarity, she stood at the doorway of creation itself. *How can I destroy this? How can I even contemplate changing it in any way?*

The beauty of the skies, with their endless possibilities, clashed with the looming threat of annihilation, creating a moment suspended between creation and oblivion.

Time suspended around Alicia, lost in that singular moment. She swam in the thoughts of her actions; her past actions, her hatred, her love, her power, everything she had ever done condensed into this one moment.

An overwhelming feeling of love swamped every part of her mind, feelings, and thoughts, and she swam in a wave of deep connection with everything around her.

Iain faded into the background as she rode this amazing wave.

Her body was everywhere now, not just standing at the edge of the Lake. She was all the universes. She was the creator, the light, the darkness, and everything good about human life, and she was Alicia at that very moment.

Her physical body was a grain of sand in a vast desert.

CHAPTER 22

"This is an emergency evacuation. All students, please lock on to an energy location to port back home. Can all students lock on to an energy location to port back home. You will have two minutes before we port all students back home. This is not a test. I repeat, this is not a test. All students lock on to an energy location now," the voice over the tannoy came inside their bubble.

David and Jessica looked at each other in disbelief.

"This is another test?" David asked, looking at Jessica and the other students inside the bubble.

They all looked outside and could see the skies burning.

"I somehow don't think it is. Quick, we better lock onto our homes." Said Anya.

All the students sat down, closed their eyes and locked onto the energy signatures of their homes.

David opened his eyes and whispered to Jessica, "Jess, do you want to lock on to Aunt Gen's, and we can be there together?"

Jessica thought briefly, "No, my dad will probably be at home, so I will port there first, and we can meet later."

"Okay, I'll see you soon." He said and closed his eyes again.

They both closed their eyes. David tried to calm the panic that was rising inside him.

David still entertained the idea that this was part of the test from the academy, but thinking about it more, he dismissed it.

"You have thirty seconds left. All students, please lock on to the energy signature of your homes." The tannoy voice faded into the background as David ported to his Aunt Gen's home in Glasgow.

The portal had opened, and Aunt Gen, Jonathan, his mother, and his father were all waiting for them.

When David opened his eyes, he was stepping into the living room of his Aunt Gen's house. He saw his mother and father again and stopped dead in his tracks.

This time, he wouldn't let himself get whisked away like he was the last time he had seen them.

His mother and father smiled broad smiles and rushed over to embrace him.

David was ecstatic to see them and smiled over at his Aunt Gen as he held out his hand for her.

As David pulled out of the embrace, a mixture of

elation, panic, and excitement swirled around in his mind. "What's going on? They evacuated us from the academy trials?"

Aunt Gen looked at him, "We don't know, it's all strange. I think Alicia has started her destruction of the Akashic records."

"What makes you say that?" David asked.

His mother and father looked at each other. "We were out last night, and everybody in the street is acting strange. Weirdly, none of the witches seem to be affected, which is a good thing, but it's very weird out on the streets, David," his father said.

"I am so glad you got back to us safely, but I fear we've no time to catch up. We have to find out what's happening and do something about it." his mother said, smiling at David.

"Why did Jessica not come with you?" Aunt Gen asked.

"She's going back to her home to check on her dad. I imagine they'll both come over once they've met up," David replied.

"Well, we think Terence has had a great idea, but he hasn't got back to us yet to implement it. It's about raising the energy of the world population." David's mother said, trying hard to get to the business at hand, but David was an enormous distraction for her.

A whooshing sound stopped the conversation.

Everyone waited nervously to see who was going to appear. It was Terence.

Terence looked up at David. "The wanderer returns. It's good to see you back with us, David. I've missed you."

David shook his head in disbelief, "My god, are you showing some love, T?"

Terence rolled his eyes, "Up your hole." he shot back.

David burst out laughing as David's mother and father frowned at the exchange between their son and this strange creature.

David, still laughing, said, "It's okay, we've got a lot of history." as an explanation for Terence's banter.

David looked down at Terence, who raised his wing. David swiped his hand on Terence's wing to give an interspecies high-five.

He'd missed Terence and the banter between them.

Another whooshing sound interrupted them again.

"My goodness, it's like Glasgow Central here today." Aunt Gen said. Everyone laughed and turned toward the giant glowing circle.

Jessica and Joseph stepped out.

Jessica smiled at David and hugged Aunt Gen, Jonathan, David's mother, and father. She looked down to wink at Terence. She didn't have the time to get a proper introduction to David's mother and father.

Joseph looked serious as he said his hellos to everyone, shaking hands with Jacqueline and Logan when Genevieve introduced them. "Good to meet you." he said and then looked at Genevieve, "We have a big problem,"

Aunt Gen nodded, "We know. We felt the shift. Jacqueline and Logan have been out, and something weird is happening."

"What do you mean by weird?" Joseph asked.

"Well, people are walking around in a daze just now. They are functioning and talking, but something is missing. I can't quite explain it." Logan said.

Joseph nodded, "It might be worse than we thought. Iain Fraser attacked Alicia Collins, and I will bet he's behind what's happening just now. There's a shift in consciousness, probably happening worldwide."

Terence said, "So, we must implement this plan as soon as possible."

"What plan," David and Jessica asked at the same time.

Terence gave Joseph, David and Jessica the details of his plan.

CHAPTER 23

Alicia stood at the lake's edge when the connection to the universe stopped for her abruptly and pulled her back down to the seventh plane with a bang.

She felt something profound, something she could only describe in her mind as being part of the universe, but she was also physically part of the universe at the same time.

She now looked at Iain. He wanted to destroy the Akashic records for whatever reason, but she couldn't figure out why. *Did he have the same plan as her? Did he know how to install a different version? Could someone install a new version?*

She wondered if it could be done. As she stood looking over at Iain, she thought about her plans and realised that what she was doing was absurd. It wasn't just absurd; it was wrong on so many levels. What the hell was she *even thinking about?*

She felt sad as she watched Iain and could sense what he planned.

Something had happened to her. She couldn't quite explain what it was, but she had connected with something much more profound than herself. Now, her plans sounded like the plans of a madwoman. Now, the problem was what she did about Iain.

Alicia felt lost in her thoughts when Iain walked over to her with a maniacal grin spread across his face.

"Have you figured it out yet?" Iain asked her.

"Figured what out? I don't know what you are planning." Alicia asked, trying to understand Iain with her newfound awareness.

"I want to destroy the Akashic records, just like you, but for different reasons, and I have a much better understanding of how to do it," Iain said, looking more like himself again.

"But you won't be able to install a new version of the Akashic records. I thought I could do that, but I don't have the power or the knowledge. Now, I am not even inclined to do it. How are you going to manage it?" Alicia said. She was building up her inner defences to protect herself against Iain should this come to some kind of battle.

"That's the difference between me and you, Alicia. You were doing it for all the wrong reasons. Deep down, you were a humanitarian, just like your father. You wanted a better world, a world where men didn't have control over everything and a world where equality ruled. I don't," Iain said, sitting down as if they were having a friendly chat.

Alicia shook her head in disbelief. The fate of the human population rested on what they were doing right now, and here Iain is sitting down. "So, what is it you want?"

Iain looked up at her, "Control. You see, I discovered that non-witches were under the influence of the Akashic records. Their entire identity stems from the knowledge passed down for centuries. As I told you when I last saw you, there is another energy source called The Nexus of Dreams."

Alicia now sat beside him as she wanted to hear what he said. The rage that she would have normally felt was just not there. In a moment, she had gone from someone full of hatred, anger, and rage to someone where there was no hatred or anger; she just was Alicia Collins. Her identity seemed a bit disconnected now, as she had wrapped her identity up with someone powerful, someone angry, someone full of hatred for men. She now understood the origins of her anger and hatred and how misplaced it had been. Alicia would now have to atone for the atrocities that she had committed. She didn't know what the atonement would look like. Right now, someone else hadn't had the same flash of insight she had, and she would have to deal with it.

She looked at Iain, "So you drain the Lake of Enlightenment. What's next?"

Iain laughed, "There is no, what next. It will be a world full of witches, and we don't need non-witches, so we can control them in a much better way than we currently do. You've been using the media to control everyone's emotions worldwide, creating fear, which lowers the energy of the human population. I am saying there's a much easier way."

Alicia looked at Iain and raised her eyebrows.

"So, all we need to do now is whisper to the Akashic records something we want all non-witches to feel, and it will be done, as long as we keep them on the same energy signature they have just now. You and many other media moguls have done an amazing job in dropping non-witches' energy signatures. Now, I have a plug-in that can control them even faster and faster than any media corporation can do, as long as their energy signature stays at the same level." Iain said as he smiled at the simplicity of his plan.

"You're forgetting that most witches are good people, and they would never accept you in the world with your manipulation of the non-witches," Alicia said as she stood up.

Iain quickly stood up next to her. "None of the other witches will know what I can do. I needed you to show me how to manipulate the Akashic records, and you've done that, so I am afraid you've outlived your usefulness."

"Oh, so you're going to kill me, are you?" Alicia asked.

"Yes! Yes, that's exactly what I am going to do. You led me here, and I am truly grateful for that, but I now know all I need to know. I have additional power from the Nexus of Dreams, something else I can effectively tap into when I need it, so you can never stop me."

As Alicia raised her defences even more whilst letting Iain waffle on about his powers, there was a sudden flash in the skies of the universes above.

They both looked up at the skies and realised it was coming from the Lake of Enlightenment. The lake was filling up again, glowing with a bright silver light emanating from the water-like substance.

CHAPTER 24

I t had been 2 hours since Terence had disappeared and asked them to wait on him. He asked Jacqueline and Logan to go back out onto Byres Road again in a few hours to get a feel for the mood of the area.

As they waited on Terence, David and Jessica asked how it would work.

David now understood how easy it was to manipulate human energy, so he got the gist of what Terence had told them. By sending out a frequency that was offset with the frequency they were currently on, the two signals clashed together to form another frequency. This new frequency would, if Terence's plan went according to his theory, raise the energy of the non-witches.

"So, why does this frequency change that Terence is

doing not affect witches," David asked, trying to understand as much as possible.

Joseph cleared his throat, "It's because witches are already on a higher frequency than non-witches, so what Terence is doing will not affect us as much. We were born with a different energy signature than non-witches, hence the reason we have special powers."

Joseph had asked Terence to accompany him to help Terence implement his plan, but Terence had refused. He would do advanced multi-location with his astral powers, meaning he would be in multiple places simultaneously. This would help him test his plans on a relatively large scale. He could then port over to the Lake of Enlightenment to discover what would happen.

Jessica was reading a book about multi-location that Aunt Gen had on her bookshelves. It looked as if no one had touched it in years. David looked through the other books on the shelves with renewed interest. He hadn't paid attention to all Aunt Gen's books, but now he had been to the academy and was still in study mode. His brain was much more receptive to everything around him.

Books were now a source of nourishment for his mind and something to look forward to instead of feeling dread at having to read for knowledge. The academy had opened his mind, and he had grown in so many ways, but his thirst for knowledge was the most significant difference he had noticed. He realised that obsession was the first step to mastery of any subject, and he had become obsessed with Magick in all its forms.

He stole a glance at Jessica as she curled up on the couch with her feet tucked under her thighs and the book resting on one leg. He quickly looked away when she looked up at him.

"Your book is upside down." She said, laughing at him.

David looked at the book and realised it wasn't. She was just telling him she had caught him. He smiled and opened Energy Frequencies of the Magickal Practitioner.

The rest of the group were talking in the kitchen area.

To David, this felt like the calm before the storm. He wanted to be as calm as possible for any eventuality over the next few hours. David was also interested in the topic in the book and ran his hand over the red leather cover, which was embossed with a brass-like metallic symbol that looked Indian.

He flipped the large book cover open and ran his finger down the chapter titles:

1. Introduction to Energy Frequencies and the Magickal Path
2. Harmonising with the Natural World: Tuning into Earth's Vibrations
3. The Human Aura: Understanding Your Energetic Signature

4. Raising and Directing Energy: Techniques and Practices

5. The Elemental Forces: Engaging with Earth, Air, Fire, Water, and Spirit

6. Chakras: Gateways of Power and Transformation

7. The Power of the Moon: Working with Lunar Cycles

8. Sacred Spaces and Energy Vortexes: Creating and Harnessing Power

9. Crystals and Stones: Amplifiers of Magickal Energy

10. Herbs and Plants: Vibrational Allies in Magickal Work

11. Symbols and Sigils: Encoding Intentions within Energy Patterns

12. Rituals and Ceremonies: Structuring Energy for Magickal Outcomes

13. Sound and Vibration: The Magick of Music and Chanting

14. Psychic Defence: Shielding and Protecting Your Energy

15. Astral Projection and Etheric Travel: Navigating the Energy Realms

16. Connecting with Spirit Guides and Deities: Enhancing Your Energetic Network

17. Divination and Intuition: Interpreting Energy Signals

He wanted to feel which chapter excited him the most. As he looked at the chapter titles, one jumped out immediately: *Sound and Vibration: The Magick of Music and Chanting.*

He started reading it immediately, and the words quickly engrossed him:

This chapter unveils the ancient understanding that sound, at its core, is vibration, and these vibrations have the power to shape reality itself. Through the deliberate use of music and chanting, practitioners can align their energy frequencies with the universe's natural rhythms, facilitating transformation, healing, and manifestation.

The chapter begins by exploring the foundational concept that sound created the universe, citing various cultural myths and modern scientific theories that support the notion of the cosmos as a symphony of vibrational frequencies. It discusses how every object, thought, and entity vibrates at its specific frequency and how these frequencies interact to create the tapestry of our experienced reality.

Delving deeper, the chapter thoroughly examines how music and chanting can alter vibrations within the practitioner's aura and the surrounding environment. It explains that by handpicking musical tones and rhythms or by chanting specific mantras and affirmations, a practitioner can elevate their vibrational state, clear energetic blockages, and attract desired outcomes. The book highlights the power of these sound vibrations as a crucial element in achieving specific Magickal goals.

This book offers practical guidance on sound and vibration in daily magickal practice. Techniques such as creating personalised chants, using instruments in rituals, and employing the human voice as a tool of enchantment are discussed. The chapter emphasises the importance of understanding different sounds' unique and spiritual resonance, encouraging readers to experiment with and intuitively select sounds that align with their magickal intentions.

"The Magick of Music and Chanting" also addresses the communal aspect of sound in magick, exploring how group chanting and collective musical performances can amplify energetic intentions and create a unified field of consciousness. This shared vibrational space facilitates more profound connections between practitioners, enhances the power of ritual work, and links the magickal community to the cosmic dance of the universe.

In closing, this chapter invites readers to embrace sound

and vibration as vital components of their magickal toolkit. By mastering music and chanting, practitioners can unlock additional dimensions of power, healing, and transformation, weaving their desires into the fabric of reality through the magick of sound.

David heard a voice on the periphery of his consciousness, but he was so engrossed in the text that when Jessica called over to him, he did not consciously hear her until the 3rd or 4th time.

Jessica had jumped up from the couch, "It's time, come on."

"Shit." David put the book down and stood up, "Wait, time for what?"

He followed Jessica into the kitchen area where Aunt Gen, His mother, father, and Joseph sat.

"Whatever Terence is doing, is working. We've just returned from Byres Road, and it's just like normal. Everybody going about their business, happier it would seem. There's a lot of singing and laughter from Ashton Lane, which I imagine is unusual for a Wednesday night." Logan said.

"So what do we do now, just wait on Terence?" David asked, bending down to tie the laces of his trainers to prepare for going somewhere.

"Yes. I imagine he will want us all to help him somehow. He said other monks are helping him, too, so we'll see when he gets back."

Just then, they heard the circle opening up in the living room. They all walked through to wait for

Terence to return and mentally prepared themselves to go into action.

As they stood at the other end of the living room, waiting for Terence, seeing someone else entering the living room instead of Terence shocked them. Joseph readied himself for defence, as did Jacqueline and Logan.

CHAPTER 25

"Is this something to do with you?" Iain asked, turning to look at her.

"I have nothing to do with this," Alicia said almost unconsciously.

He turned back toward the Lake.

Alicia looked at him and felt sorry for him, and she knew that killing was the right thing to do and letting him live was the right thing to do. These were two opposing ideas, a cognitive dissonance that would never work on the earth plane. Ultimately, it was a choice; she could choose to try to kill him and feel love for him or choose to let him live and feel love for him. These were all strange ideas that floated around in Alicia's head, and it was hard for her to understand what was happening.

Her conscious mind was battling with the mind of the universe.

How do you make a choice when something is neither right nor wrong?

Alicia knew this connection with the universe, or all the universes that exist, was not a connection. She was the universe.

She struggled to bring her mind back to this individual body that she currently inhabited.

Iain glanced at her sceptically, doubting her claim of innocence as the Lake of Enlightenment appeared to stir back to life once more.

Alicia could already feel the shift in energy; it felt like a heaviness had lifted from her.

She knew the non-witches on the Earth plane would feel this, too, but they wouldn't know what was causing this feeling.

Iain stood at the edge of the Lake and held his hands over it. He was trying to pull the energy from the Lake through him. She watched him, fascinated by what he was doing and what he was hoping to achieve. She just let him carry on to see what would come of it. Whatever happened would be something that happened at this moment. Somewhere else, in an alternate universe, he and she might do something different that would lead to a different outcome, and that, too, would be the right thing to do at that moment.

She watched as the Lake gave up some of its energy to Iain. As soon as the Lake dimmed in brightness, it seemed to fill again and glow even brighter. Alicia could tell Iain was getting frustrated as he stood with his hands held over the lake's edge.

He was now chanting over and over.

O aquae vitae, fontem sapientiae, ad me transfer tuam potentiam.

Luminis essentia, ex tenebris ad lucem me duc.

Per hanc invocatio, viribus naturae, mihi concede quod quaero.

Fluxum energiae ab imo lacus ad animam meam permitti.

Alicia immediately translated the Latin into her native language. She had never really grasped Latin at school, but now she understood it perfectly. She then realised she understood all languages.

O water of life, fountain of wisdom, transfer your power to me.

Essence of light, from darkness lead me to light.

By this invocation, by the forces of nature, grant me what I seek.

Allow the flow of energy from the depths of the lake to my soul.

She watched again as the power flowed through Iain and dimmed the light from the lake. Once again, the light shone brighter after a few seconds.

Iain turned to Alicia, angry and frustrated.

She smiled warmly and let him simmer in his anger.

She could feel he thought she was mocking him and lashed out at her with an energy rush.

The impact catapulted Alicia's body through the air,

but she felt nothing. As her physical body fell to the ground, she could see the bone in her arm snapping and felt the tear in her muscles as she landed awkwardly. She was the blood that rushed through her body to repair itself. The white blood cells rushed to the damaged parts of her body, and she could feel the connection to the white and red blood cells as they healed her. She was in the hospital of her own body, and she was witnessing it firsthand, not feeling pain, but she watched as neurons fired all over her body, telling her brain about the injuries she had sustained.

Iain walked over to her slowly and prepared to lash out again at her.

Alicia still felt ambivalent about him. He was a speck of dust that could cause her no harm. She observed him, fascinated, as she was being assimilated into the universal mind.

Part of her, the human conscious part, was trying to understand how all this was happening. The other part of her mind was observing.

Time was no longer time, as each microsecond lasted as long as it should last, which might be forever or never.

Her body healed almost as quickly as the impact injured her. The communication between her mind, or the universal mind, with every organ in her physical body was instantaneous. She stood up and let Iain blast her again with a powerful force.

He couldn't understand what was happening and

why her physical body was not dying with the brutal force he was blasting her with.

Each time, she stood up and smiled.

Alicia then felt the surrounding energy changing. There were more witches about to come to the seventh plane.

She looked at Iain, who was now red with the rage, anger and fury burning inside him.

She could feel what he was feeling. He was angry at her for not dying at this moment, angry at life at not having enough power, raging with a life that had left him bereft of power ever since he had been a young boy. He now craved power and control in every aspect of his life. She felt it all without having to understand it.

She would let whatever happened happen and took no part in the outcome.

CHAPTER 26

A man with a smile as wide as the Clyde walked through and looked at everyone.

"Aarif!" Gasped Jessica, "What are you doing here?"

Still smiling and clearly glad to be helping, Aarif looked at Jessica. "Terence has asked me to help you port to the seventh plane and given me this so we can get to the exact spot." He held up a glass object that sparkled with a gold liquid substance inside.

"I don't understand," Jessica said, stepping toward him, "Why you if you're on the second level?"

Aarif bowed his head a little, "I am a monk, helping Terence look after you and David on your journey. When I met you in the Library of Life, I knew you'd be there and knew what I must do to help you."

Jessica looked at David and laughed, "So you've been helping us all this time?" Jessica asked.

"Well, Terence and I have been looking out for you, shall we say? But we have little time. There is already some activity on the seventh plane. You must follow me through the portal, but hold on to each other as you go through." He looked at all the faces in the room again as if taking a head count. He gave a slight nod and motioned for them to go through the portal, with David and Jessica going first, holding onto Aarif's shoulder.

As everyone formed a human chain, they all walked through the portal.

Jessica stepped out of the portal into a darkened mountainous terrain and immediately saw the glow of the Lake of Enlightenment. The port had been almost instantaneous this time, and she wondered what the gold-like substance Aarif held was. That was a question for another time.

They were all there: Jessica, David, Joseph, Aunt Gen, Jonathan, Jacqueline, Logan and Aarif.

Aarif looked at them, "I will be back soon, but right now," he pointed to where Alicia and Iain Fraser stood, "This is the time and place where someone will either destroy or save the Akashic records." He turned to them, smiled and then walked back through the portal, which winked out of existence instantly.

"What on earth does that mean," Joseph said, leading the way as they walked around the edge of the Lake of Enlightenment to where Alicia and Iain were.

Jacqueline and Logan broke out in a run when they saw Iain unleash another strike on Alicia.

Iain then turned to them as he saw them approaching. Momentarily confused, he looked at Jacqueline and Logan and then back to Alicia. He closed his eyes briefly as if summoning more energy and then let rip a barrage of strikes on Jacqueline and Logan.

Logan jumped from behind Jacqueline, and now, side by side, they shielded off the lightning strikes with an invisible shield. The bolt of lightning travelled through the shield and still blasted them back a few feet. The shield absorbed the blast's worst, but Jacqueline and Logan lay injured on the ground.

David let out a strike of his own after watching his mother and father being attacked.

Surprised again at seeing David, Iain fell back slightly as his left shoulder had taken a hit.

Sparks appeared before him and started flying about like millions of fireflies. They looked like tiny balls of fire. Iain directed the millions of tiny flames towards the oncoming group. Everyone stopped and instinctively shielded themselves. The first hit from the balls of fire hit against the shields of everyone there, but they snaked their way around the shield and attacked from all angles.

Aunt Gen screamed out in Agony as the tiny fireballs attacked her, and part of her clothing was alight. Jonathan quickly created a force field around them and helped Aunt Gen put out fire-lit clothes. They were busy swatting more of the fireballs that were inside the shield.

Jessica and Joseph flanked Iain. Jessica threw a wave of water over him that she hoped would momentarily confuse and disable him. As she did this and Joseph saw what his daughter was doing, he then lifted his hands to form a mini hurricane, which pulled up rocks and sand from the floor of the terrain and forced them toward Iain.

The water barrage hit Iain first, and Jessica was right. It stunned him for a second or two. He quickly gathered his composure and prepared to unleash something else on them. He was then hit squarely with the mini hurricane that Joseph had created. This worked. He was thrown back off his feet and swept up in the hurricane.

Joseph checked on the others.

David had rushed toward his Aunt Gen to make sure she was okay. Jonathan was taking care of her. David seemed satisfied his Aunt Gen was okay and ran toward Jessica's side.

Jessica looked at her father, nodded, and walked toward Iain and Alicia.

Alicia was watching all this happen and didn't move to do anything. Jessica thought she must be waiting until they disposed of Iain before Alicia made a move on them.

Jessica ignored Alicia for now and prepared to battle with Iain's immediate threat, but he had now disappeared. The mini tornado Joseph had created had swept him up, and now he was nowhere to be seen.

David stepped up beside Jessica as the others looked around for Iain.

Suddenly, a blanket of darkness fell over them. All the light had disappeared, and they were now shrouded in darkness.

Jessica shouted out, "Is everyone okay."

There were replies from everyone, but they all said they couldn't see anything.

Jessica felt a low rumbling sound around her, which was getting louder. Her legs started shaking as the noise reverberation seemed to hit her. It was like her bones were being shaken from the inside. *What the fuck is this?* She asked herself as the noise grew louder and the reverberation travelled up her body. She heard Aunt Gen screaming, and then she could hear her father stifling a scream by moaning loudly and trying to fight whatever it was.

"Jess," She barely heard as David tried to shout. "The grounding spell, the grounding spell," he said before his voice trailed off. Jessica didn't know what he was talking about as the noise had fully gripped her body, and she vibrated from head to toe. She felt as if her brain was shaking inside her head, hitting against the walls of her skull. She couldn't think straight. *Grounding spell, grounding spell,* she said, trying to hold on to the thought. Then it clicked.

Immediately, she remembered being taught the spell in Mesopotamia.

She imagined herself burrowing deep into the

earth's core, spinning as she went to reach the very centre of the earth. They had been told this would help them reconnect with themselves and ward off spells used against them.

She was still shaken from the inside out, but it was slowing down now, and she could think more clearly. She tried harder and harder to think of herself burrowing into the earth's core.

Finally, the head rattling stopped, and Jessica could see again. Her eyes rolled around on the landscape as she fought to keep her focus.

She saw David had successfully stopped the shaking, and he was with his Aunt Gen, holding her as Jonathan stood close by.

Her father, too, seemed to be okay. He tried to run toward Iain but stumbled and fell over, obviously still disoriented from the rattling.

Jacqueline and Logan were holding onto each other and looked okay.

Jessica locked eyes with David and briefly nodded as they knew what to do.

CHAPTER 27

T erence sat in a circle with the three other monks. Together, they helped the Earth plane despite not knowing what would happen to them when the elders found out.

Together, they focused on a white ball of energy that hovered before them. This was the energy source that they were using to tap into the earth's energy and change it to a higher frequency. They had been sitting for a long time, gathering their energy to merge with this new wave of energy and push it out into the Earth plane.

They could feel it was working, but they knew Alicia would try to halt their efforts by destroying the Akashic records. It became a tug-of-war, not a battle of good versus evil, but a clash of differing perspectives.

The four monks sat on top of the Earth plane and focused on seeking the radio, television, and mobile signals that were snaking their way worldwide like a web. They then used the energy from the white ball in the middle of their circle to inject the new signal.

They didn't speak, open their eyes, or feel. They just used their minds to focus their attention on injecting the new signal that would travel throughout the entire world. Current technology would help speed this up.

As the monks continued their silent vigil, the white ball of energy pulsed with an ever-increasing glow, a visual testament to their deep concentration and task potency. With each pulse, waves of refined energy cascaded through the invisible networks of the Earth plane, intertwining with the communication signals of human creation. This fusion, although unseen, wove a new tapestry of consciousness across the globe that people would feel profoundly.

In every corner of the Earth, humanity would be attuned to this shift in energy. People would pause, mid-conversation, mid-thought, feeling an inexplicable lightness, a sudden clarity of mind that cut through the fog of daily existence. The air they breathed daily would now carry whispers of awakening, nudging humanity towards a collective evolution.

The monks remained steadfast, a conduit for this monumental change. They understood the delicate balance of their actions; doing too much too soon could overwhelm people, and doing too little could mean their efforts got lost in the noise of daily life. It was a symphony of energy they orchestrated, each note carefully placed among the currents of technology.

The world outside their circle remained oblivious to the source of this sudden shift. They would meet in their virtual worlds and talk about this strange shift that seemed to happen. Others would meet online and talk in forums, and more would come together in cafes, living rooms, and social clubs and talk to each other again. A sense of unity would bridge divides that had previously seemed insurmountable.

They would realise that a handful of extremely rich and connected people controlled the world they were living in. They would understand that their governments were not acting for the benefit of the many but for the benefit of the few. People would come together with new ideas on how to govern the world, help each other, and rid the world of poverty, hunger and war. Eventually, the monks could see it all happening; it was within reach of the Earth plane inhabitants, and it felt right to do what they were doing. They knew it wouldn't happen overnight, but they were part of the catalyst that could make it happen, eventually.

However, the monks knew their actions would not go unnoticed in the realms beyond. Forces, both supportive and adversarial, would watch closely. The stakes were high, for altering the course of human evolution was no small feat. It was a gambit that could redefine the fabric of existence on the Earth plane and beyond.

As the monks continued their focused attention on the Earth's energy signature, they knew it might all count for nothing if Alicia and other forces destroyed the Akashic records. For this, they relied on the Witches of Scotland to save the Akashic records, and for now, more than ever, the very fabric of human existence sat on the shoulders of the Witches.

CHAPTER 28

David rushed over to Jessica.

In the thick veil of darkness and in the silence of the Seventh plane, Jessica and David understood the urgency of their next move. Their eyes met, and an unspoken agreement passed between them. It was time to use the ancient spell they had discovered together while training with Aleister Crowley.

David clearly remembered the incantation, and Jessica nodded to him, showing she knew what to do.

David began his voice steady, "Elements of the cosmos, hear our plea," calling upon the universal forces that govern balance and harmony.

Jessica joined him, "From the depth of Earth to the breadth of Sky, lend us the strength to protect and preserve." Their words wove together, a symphony of intent and power.

They chanted, "By the sacred bond that unites all life, shield these records from harm and strife. Let not this darkness consume our light; safeguard the Akashic with all our might."

The ground beneath their feet thrummed with energy, the air crackled, and the darkness receded like a tide pulling away from the shore. The Lake of Enlightenment seemed to respond, its glow intensifying, casting long, dancing shadows across the mountainous terrain.

As their incantation reached its crescendo, a shimmering golden light lit the dark skies. The Akashic records were briefly visible as images of billions of people glowed brightly in the skies. Memories of the dead, the ancients, and those yet to be born took to the skies in a dance, like a kaleidoscope of dreams, weaving through the night with ethereal grace. These haunting and beautiful visions painted the heavens with the stories of time itself, echoing the eternal cycle of life, death, and rebirth. Each twirl and swirl of this celestial ballet held whispers of wisdom passed down through ages, a testament to the enduring spirit of existence that connects the past, present, and future in an unbreakable chain of being.

David and Jessica, still holding hands, lifted their etheric bodies into the Akashic records and merged them with the cacophony of dreams. They were now a part of the past, present and future.

Iain appeared again on the other side of the Lake,

watching the spectacle. He did not have the power to do anything at this moment.

A light rain fell over the seventh plane, composed of white light cascading from the Akashic records.

A sudden flash caused all the Witches to turn around. It was a portal that was opening up. As everyone prepared for another battle, the faces of Aunt Gen's group appeared one by one: Myra, Alistair, Caroline, Sanjeev, Lillian, and the others had all come to help the Witches on their quest to save the Akashic records.

Jessica and David's energy circled above as the skies were still aglow with the billions of faces, thoughts, memories and images of the Akashic records.

The rest of the group, except Jacqueline and Logan, formed a circle as David and Jessica's etheric bodies joined them in the centre. They reached out to each group member and helped them unify their spirits in a common goal.

Iain tried his hardest to use his magick on the group as they travelled from their physical bodies into the astral realm. It was useless. He could not use his magick. He turned quickly, hearing Jacqueline and Logan behind him.

Jacqueline was first to strike, and Logan struck shortly after to cut off the magickal energy surrounding Iain. Iain, surprised by the sudden surge of protective energy, faltered. His schemes, so carefully laid, unravelled in the face of such unified resistance. The blanket of darkness lifted entirely.

Iain didn't speak and accepted his fate. He had tried to destroy something natural and previously thought to be immutable. In his quest for power, he had underestimated the collective strength and resolve of those standing before him. The group, now fully aligned in purpose and spirit, watched as the ethereal light from their united force enveloped Iain, cleansing the area of his malicious intent and restoring balance. This moment was not just a victory over Iain but a reaffirmation of their dedication to preserving the sanctity of the magical realms and the natural order. As Iain vanished into the void, a sense of peace settled over them, but there was another person to deal with. The person who had started it all was Alicia Collins.

CHAPTER 29

S till a wildcard in the unfolding drama, Alicia watched from a distance. The intensity of Jessica and David's spell work and the clarity of their purpose gave her pause. For a moment, the future of the Akashic records and all they represented hung in the balance, safeguarded by the very individuals she had underestimated.

Fully recovered and emboldened by their success, the group rallied around Jessica and David. They knew the battle was far from over, but they found renewed strength and determination in this moment of victory over Iain. The fight to protect the Akashic records had united them in ways they could never have expected, forging bonds that the trials to come would test.

Alicia stood before the group and didn't speak. She had stood back and watched the Akashic records nearly being destroyed, and she had been the one to instigate it. She would accept whatever fate was about to befall her. There was no need to protect herself. She was now a part of the Akashic records in a much different way than she had first expected.

The overwhelming feeling of love that had engulfed her earlier had come directly from the Akashic records, and the thought of even trying to destroy it was now strange to her.

She wondered if she could return to the Earth plane. Knowing what she knew now would make her a different person. Alicia didn't feel the overwhelming love that she had experienced before, but she now possessed knowledge that no other human, witch or non-witch, would have access to. How would she use it, she wondered?

Then she felt it.

A surge throughout her whole body as Jacqueline and Logan unleashed an attack on her. She looked at them, their determined, angry faces. They did not know that the experience had forever changed her. All they knew was that the Alicia Collins of the Earth plane was an evil, egotistical, powerful, controlling witch who had nearly destroyed the whole of humanity and had thought nothing about it. She had played dice with 8 billion people living on Earth like she rolled the dice as if they were mere chips in her high-stakes game of cosmic roulette. Each roll, each toss into the chaotic whirlwind of fate, risked altering the fabric of existence for countless souls. It was a game played in the shadows of destiny, where the stakes were not just her ambitions but humanity's collective destiny.

She knew she deserved destruction and would not attempt to convince The Witches of Scotland otherwise.

A spell that would not kill her struck her again.

A strange sensation coursed through her body. The fabric of her soul was being pulled apart into millions of pieces scattered into the cosmic winds of the Akashic records.

David and Jessica watched, knowing that this would be the right thing to do.

They wouldn't kill Alicia Collins. They would let her be part of the solution to change the situation on the Earth plane: the corruption, greed, famine, poverty, and imbalances between the greedy and the poor. She would become a part of the Akashic records herself, with a voice that would whisper help when required. She would become a ghost in the machine of life.

Alicia felt David and Jessica as she journeyed from her physical body to the energetic force of the Akashic records.

She whispered to David, "I will always be here. Just reach out."

Alicia took a last deep breath of physical air as her astral body blended with the collective consciousness. A brief burst of light lit up the skies of the seventh plane as a powerful witch joined the collective consciousness.

CHAPTER 30

David and Jessica gently re-entered their physical bodies on the seventh plane and watched Alicia Collins melt into the skies above.

David looked around for his mother and father, who were now grinning and walking toward them. He looked over for his Aunt Gen, and she too was okay, as was the large group that had stood with them to save the Akashic records.

Jessica and David looked at each other and finally breathed an enormous sigh of relief. Their quest to save the Akashic records had worked. The enormity of what they had done, with the help of the Witches of Scotland, would never truly hit them.

They looked out over the Lake of Enlightenment, now glowing brightly. The vapour of white light had risen sharply.

They all turned with the sound of a portal opening close by.

It was Terence and the three monks. Terence was now in his monk form, not the little creature that David and Jessica knew and loved. Despite looking physically different, they knew it was Terence. His energetic presence was just the same as the creature they knew.

Terence smiled at Jessica and David and embraced Jessica and then David, filling them immediately with a strange feeling of love, which David could only describe as a deep connection.

He looked at them and then turned to look at everyone in the group.

"I may see none of you again, as what we have done here," he said, pointing to the other three monks, "We should not have done. This is the first time any monk from the seventh plane has ever interfered with what was happening on the Earth plane. We still stand by our decision, and we will take the consequences of our actions, but those consequences will not affect you as the inhabitants of the Earth plane. Thank you for what you have done. You will never truly understand what you have accomplished. I would also like to say, personally, I have enjoyed getting to know all of you." He looked at Aunt Gen and smiled affectionately at her. He then turned to Jessica and David.

Jessica and David stepped up to him.

"You two have been a monumental pain in the arse, but I have enjoyed every minute of your company. May this be just the start of your magickal journey together. I know and have seen what you will do, and you both should feel proud of yourselves for the journey you have been on."

David felt like he was saying goodbye to a lifelong friend, and tears started rolling down his cheeks. He didn't know if he would see Terence again, but he realised this journey had culminated in the saving of the Akashic records. From his boring life as a law student at Glasgow University to this, a powerful Witch who had grown from a boy into a man. He had finally got to see his mother and father after nineteen years. And, he had found a great friend, or something more, in Jessica Campbell, and he had found his place in the world. He now belonged to a group known as the Witches of Scotland.

Jessica looked at him, who also had tears streaming down her cheeks as Terence spoke. She held out her hand.

David took it and smiled.

It was time to go back to the Earth plane.

He watched as Jessica spoke to her father. The immense love he felt for her at that moment was overwhelming.

He then looked at his mother and father, who were beaming with pride.

At last, he got to hug them—not just a hug of hello, but a hug of a lifelong hope that he had harboured. The embrace was emotional, and he didn't want to stop holding them.

As he was hugging his parents, he looked over at his Aunt Gen. Jonathan had wrapped his arms around her. She smiled warmly at him and touched her hand to her heart area. David whispered I love you to her. She buried her head in Jonathan's chest. Jonathan held out his fist to David and nodded to him, acknowledging the man he had become within the space of a year.

He looked at Aunt Gen's group of witches and smiled, knowing how much they had risked and how many stories they would have to tell their grandchildren.

It was now hitting him. The enormity of what had just happened was punching him square in the chest.

It was time to go home.

EPILOGUE

David and Jessica were lounging in Aunt Gen's living room, discussing what had happened over the last few months.

It had been two days since they had saved the Akashic records from being destroyed. They had not expected it would be Iain Fraser they would be battling.

"Do you not find it strange that Alicia didn't put up any kind of fight?" Jessica asked, not expecting an answer.

"Mm, I've thought about it a lot." David sat up straight, "Do you remember when she whispered, 'I will always be here, just reach out'?"

Jessica looked at him. "You've tried to reach out to her, haven't you?" she said, smiling.

David laughed, "Well, I did, half-heartedly, though, but I genuinely got the feeling that something had happened to her that made her change her mind about destroying the Akashic records."

Jessica nodded, "Yeah, I know what you mean. Are you feeling well rested?"

David frowned, "What do you mean?" he asked, looking over at her.

Jessica smiled seductively.

"Oh, that kind of rested, then yes, I am rested." He said, crawling over to her on the couch.

Just then, Aunt Gen walked in with Jonathan.

"Oh, sorry, I hope I'm not disturbing anything." She said just as David was about to launch himself onto Jessica.

David quickly swung around and sat up on the couch. "No, no, not at all. We were just talking about Alicia and everything that's happened over the last few months."

Jonathan looked at them and smiled.

"Yes, I can imagine you have a lot to talk about. Is everything okay with your father, Jessica? This will also be a lot for him to take in."

Jessica sat up now. "Yeah, he's fine, but it all bewildered him. Strangely, though, I think he's going to miss Alicia. She was on his level in a lot of ways, and I know they looked out for each other. She helped to find me when that group kidnapped me."

"Yes. It's a strange one with Alicia. I thought I would feel no remorse about what we did to her on the

Seventh plane, but I do. I'm still wrestling with it, to be honest." Aunt Gen said, looking out of the window.

"Aunt Gen, she was gambling with the lives of every human being on Earth. She needed to be stopped." David said.

"I know, I know, but I still feel bad." She said, smiling at David for his placatory comments.

Jonathan took hold of Aunt Gen's hand and squeezed it. "So, how do you feel after finishing the magick academy?" Jonathan asked, changing the subject.

"Well, technically, we didn't finish it," Jessica said and looked at David, "Do you think we'll get to finish it?"

"Nah! We don't need to. We knew we were about to win the final battles anyway," he laughed.

They heard a knock at the door.

"That'll be Myra and Caroline. They said they were coming around later," Aunt Gen said.

Jonathan stood up, "I'll get it," he said, walking out of the living room to answer the door.

A few minutes passed as Aunt Gen, David, and Jessica were talking.

Jonathan walked into the living room slowly and looked at David and Jessica, "There's someone here to see you,"

David, Jessica and Aunt Gen looked up.

Jonathan motioned his head for Aunt Gen to leave the room with him to leave David and Jessica to it.

Aunt Gen frowned but stood up and walked to the living room door to see who it was.

A man and woman stood behind Jonathan as he led Aunt Gen away.

David and Jessica looked at each other and frowned.

David reckoned the woman was in her early thirties, and the man, in his late Forties, sat down opposite them. They dressed well and carried an air of authority and mystery that immediately set David and Jessica on edge.

"David, Jessica," the woman began, her voice clear and composed. I'm Agent Sarah Mills, and this is my colleague, Agent Mark Harrison. We're here on behalf of a covert agency tasked with investigating paranormal activities across the UK and investigating allegations of wrongdoing within large corporations and government agencies."

David and Jessica exchanged a quick, puzzled glance before Jessica asked, "What does that have to do with us?"

Agent Harrison leaned forward, "Your recent involvement with the Akashic records and the events on the Seventh Plane has not gone unnoticed. Your actions saved more than just the records; they prevented a potential catastrophe on a global scale."

Agent Mills continued, "We've been monitoring your progress for some time. Your unique talents and recent experiences make you ideal candidates for a new initiative we're launching aimed at addressing the rise in paranormal threats. We believe our worlds collide with the unseen world, and we must investigate further. The agency also needs to monitor those in power and investigate," he paused, clearing his throat slightly, "some so-called conspiracy theories. We have called it 'The Edinburgh Files.'"

"The Edinburgh Files? Why is it called that?" Jessica asked.

Agent Mills smiled, "That's where your Father is from, and he set up the task force a few years ago."

"My father? He would have told me about it." Jessica said.

"Jessica, you've already been involved in it. You stopped a potential virus from going global; that was all part of the Edinburgh Files. We collaborated with your father and set up this organisation to investigate more goings-on like this, as well as unusual paranormal activity."

David frowned, "It seems a little strange mixing conspiracy theories with paranormal activity." David said.

The two agents looked at each other. Agent Harrison said, "Well, they're not as far apart as you might think. We believe powerful witches like yourself could be behind many of these so-called conspiracy theories."

While processing the information, David asked, "What exactly do you want from us?"

"We're inviting you to join our team," Mills replied.

"With your abilities, you'll be instrumental in our operations, helping to safeguard humanity from threats most people aren't even aware exist. Of course, you'll receive training further to hone your skills and access to resources and intelligence our agency has gathered over the years. I have heard from your father how powerful you both are, so I don't imagine we can teach you much more about Magick, but we can teach you how to be excellent agents. "

Jessica, intrigued but cautious, inquired, "Are you a government agency?"

Agent Mills quipped back quickly, "Goodness no. If anything, we are investigating the government and the corruption in the corridors of power, and we would love help from you two."

Jessica seemed to like the idea of exposing corruption inside the government. "And if we agree, what then? We just leave our lives here and become... what, exactly? Agents?"

"You'll be more than just agents," Harrison assured them. "You'll be protectors, mediators between the seen and unseen. As for your lives, we understand the importance of balance. You'll still have your freedoms, but when duty calls, you need to respond."

The room fell silent as David and Jessica considered what these two agents asked. The opportunity to join an organisation like this, to use their powers for a greater purpose, was something they had never envisioned.

"Can you give us some time to think about it?" David finally asked, his gaze meeting Jessica's.

"Of course," Mills replied, standing up with Harrison. "We'll be in touch. Remember, the world is changing, and we need people like you to help guide those changes in the right direction."

With that, the agents left as quietly as they had arrived, leaving David and Jessica alone once more, their minds racing with the possibilities this fresh path could bring.

As the door closed behind the agents, Jessica turned to David, a determined glint in her eye, "Whatever we decide, we do it together. Edinburgh Files, eh? And my dad, knowing all about this, wait until I see him. But it sounds like the beginning of a new adventure."

David smiled, "As long as it's with you, I'm ready for anything."

Aunt Gen and Jonathan walked back into the living room.

"What on earth was all that about?"

David looked at Jessica.

"You might be looking at the new Mulder and Scully," David said laughing.

"What?" Aunt Gen asked.

The End of Book 8

The end of The Witches of Scotland: The Dream
Dancers: Akashic Chronicles

Discover the inspiration behind The Witches of
Scotland series in a quick video from the author Steven
and get news of his upcoming series:
https://www.stevenaitchison.co.uk/wos

CAN YOU DO ME A FAVOUR

Reviews are the most powerful tools in my little toolbox for getting attention for my books. As much as I'd like to have it, I don't have the finances the big publishers do to market my books.

However, I have something much more powerful than money: you. If you liked the book, please leave an honest review on Amazon and tell a few friends about it on social media.

You can leave a review by clicking the links below for book 1 and you can leave a review for the rest of the books too.

Amazon US: Review The Dream Dancers Book 1 in the USA

Amazon UK: Review The Dream Dancers Book 1 In UK

Amazon AUS: Review The Dream Dancers Book 1 in Australia

Amazon CAN: Review the Dream Dancers Book 1 in Canada

Also, please follow me on Amazon so you will get notified of any books I write and publish in the future.

Follow Steven Aitchison on Amazon

Thank you so much. I appreciate you.

ACKNOWLEDGMENTS

As always, I would like to thank Sharon, my amazing wife, who has always stuck by me with whatever weird and crazy schemes I have come up with. We now laugh whenever I say, "I've had an idea." I can almost see her bracing herself as I explain my next business or creative idea. Thank you for allowing me to experiment with my creative endeavours, including being a writer, artist, entrepreneur, trainer, crypto trader, Youtuber, blogger and our property development venture.

I would also like to thank my two sons for reminding me every day that I am, first and foremost, a dad and for our developing friendship as they get older.

And a huge special mention to our first grandchild, Sam, who lights up our life. Hopefully, more grandchildren will be on the way, but thank you to Sam for now.

IS THERE MORE TO COME?

Although this is the last book in this series, there will be more from David, Jess, and the rest of the Witches of Scotland's gang. I am still deciding on the storylines or the direction the new stories should take; I just know I love writing about their adventures and want to continue exploring this universe of The Witches of Scotland.

I have come up with a series entitled The Witches of Scotland: The Edinburgh Files. Please leave a comment and let me know what you think here:

The Edinburgh Files Facebook Post

·   ·   ·

If you have any other ideas, I am genuinely open to ideas, and you can write to me: authorsteven@steve naitchison.co.uk

ABOUT STEVEN AITCHISON

Steven is just an ordinary guy who likes to make up stories for a living.

He lives in the Golden Triangle, on the West End of Glasgow. When he is not writing, he loves spending most of his time with his wife, two grown sons, and family.

If you want to learn more about Steven, follow him online.

Website: www.stevenaitchison.co.uk

Email: authorsteven@stevenaitchison.co.uk

Facebook Author Page: www.facebook.com/Steven-AitchisonAuthor

Facebook main page: www.Facebook.com/ChangeYourThoughtsToday

Instagram: www.instagram.com/StevenPAitchison

Twitter: www.twitter.com/StevenAitchison

YouTube: www.YouTube.com/StevenAitchisonCYT

Printed in Great Britain
by Amazon

40963149R00126